Praise for

Victoria Blisse

This deliciously spicy novella features a fantastical scenario wherein two exceedingly wealthy men are fighting for the favors of one woman. A wonderful position to be in when it includes fabulous hotel stays, trips to exotic locations and plenty of wonderfully exciting sexual encounters. ~ *Night Owl Romance*

SHARING NICELY

VICTORIA BLISSE

Sharing Nicely
ISBN # 978-1-78184-721-3
©Copyright Victoria Blisse 2013
Cover Art by Posh Gosh ©Copyright September 2013
Interior text design by Claire Siemaszkiewicz
Totally Bound Publishing

Published in 2014 by Totally Bound Publishing, Newland House, The Point, Weaver Road, Lincoln, LN6 3QN, United Kingdom.

SHARING NICELY

Dedication

Mum, you claim to be the spark to my writing imagination and your encouragement means the world to me. Without you passing on your love of books to me, I wouldn't be an author now. Thank you.

Chapter One

My club was full of millionaires. It was terrifying. I sashayed around the room in comfortable heels and a sexy dress, smiling, when all I wanted to do was get behind the scenes to check everything was moving smoothly. But I couldn't. No, I was front of house tonight and I had to be, like it or not.

It was a dream come true to be hosting the Entrepreneur Awards. I had worked damned hard to get my club, Diamonds, up to standard. I'd started out with a huge loan that frightened me and a building crew who seemed to spend more time drinking tea than transforming my vision into reality. Eventually, though, my restaurant and bar had taken shape and it had stayed essentially the same ever since. The dance floor was the prominent feature, the tables arranged around the outside lip. People came to Diamonds to eat, drink, laugh and dance. We did have quieter cubicles at the back for those who wanted to talk with their mouths instead of their bodies and it was this balance of fun, excitement and hidey-holes that kept

Diamonds at the top of the business and one of the hottest names on the London entertainment circuit.

Happily, the chance I'd taken had paid off. I'd settled into a routine and spent every spare minute at my club. People told me it wasn't healthy, that I worked too much, but if I took time off what would I do with it? I enjoyed my work so I buried myself in it.

I liked to be in the back, checking on the chef and the wait staff, going through set lists and dealing with problems as they arose, but I knew tonight I had to be out schmoozing. The varied visitors—men and women of all ages, sizes and creeds—had more money between them than certain nations. These guests were seriously loaded. Everyone was on the rich list. The poorest were mere millionaires but the big fish like Greg Stamford and Darren Bennett were billionaires.

I wanted to book them in for tables or private functions. I wanted them to become regulars at my place. I wanted their money in my tills.

I could entertain up front like this—I could smile and flirt and sell myself and my business pretty well, but I didn't like doing it. However, it was too important tonight to pass the buck to one of my assistants. I had to do it myself.

To ease myself in, I started by chatting to a group of people gathered around a lovely couple who were regulars at Diamonds already.

"Hello, Kerry, enjoying the evening?" Sasha asked, flashing her perfect white smile beneath her expensive lipstick-soaked lips.

"As much as I can considering I'm working." I smiled. She introduced me to the people around her, including a snack food entrepreneur whose products were household staples all over the world. He was small and dumpy and had a very disconcerting habit of squeezing my thigh but before our conversation finished he'd booked a private party that would boost my profits handsomely. It was a good start to the evening.

I moved on. My cheeks ached from so many smiles, my throat was dry and I wanted to take off the stupid heels and slip into my sensible, flat everyday shoes that cradled my toes instead of crushing them. I'd only been out front for a couple of hours. The night was still young.

Taking a champagne flute from a tray as one of my waitresses passed, I looked across the crowd. Everywhere I looked there were designer dresses and suits, expensive watches and bracelets and necklaces that cost more than my annual salary to buy.

By the bar were two men who earned more a day than I did in a year. Darren Bennett and Greg Stamford were bitter rivals in the technology world. They created apps for phones and their companies had really taken over the field — spreading out into associated technologies, owning their own mobile phone networks. I was subscribed to Greg's, actually. I'd never used any of the apps they were world famous for, though. I only owned a basic mobile phone and switched it on once in a blue moon. I wasn't terribly technically minded.

Greg was tall and severe, all angles and hard lines. He was with a pretty famous model. She had to be fairly well known because even I recognized her face and I didn't buy women's magazines — they made me feel uncomfortable, as their models were so thin and elegant, the polar opposite of me. She was blonde and stick-like while he was dark. He had a caramel tan that spoke of weeks beneath exotic skies and his hair was dark black, like the classiest limousine, and equally shiny. And hot. He could take me any which way he liked, the more hostile the better.

Darren looked similar but yet completely different. He had the same elegant air and self-assured smile and stance but his hair was fiery and red. He kept it short but it curled lazily against his scalp and made him appear more relaxed. His style was more playful — even at a distance I could see he was wearing a novelty tie with a character from one of his most popular mobile games. When he laughed, which he did often and loudly, his whole face lit up.

He also had a beautiful woman beside him, a raven-haired beauty I recognized from something on the television. She was holding an in-depth conversation with Greg's model partner. The way they smiled at each other and touched led me to believe they were flirting with each other. I couldn't blame them. The men beside them, though obnoxiously rich and annoyingly handsome, hadn't shown them an ounce of interest in all the time I had watched them. They were engaged in conversation with serious men. I was sure they were working the room just as I was.

A lovely couple distracted me for a while. They wanted to find out my availability for their wedding reception. I spent a good time chatting through the options and dates with the two and when they walked off to find their table for the award ceremony I was happy in the knowledge that I'd secured a very lucrative deal indeed.

"Excuse me, would you like a drink?"

I turned and found myself looking into the startling blue eyes of Darren Bennett.

"Water would be good, thank you." I smiled.

He turned to Richard behind the bar and asked for a water and a pint of bitter for himself.

"You're the owner here, right?" he asked, returning to face me.

"Yes, I'm Kerry Matthews, nice to meet you." I offered my hand and he took it in his and shook it vigorously.

"Lovely to meet you, Kerry. I'm Darren Bennett from Bear Enterprises."

"Are you enjoying the evening so far?" I took a sip from the glass of water that had just been placed beside me. I tried to hide my nerves—even though I'd been chatting with important people all night I was a little in awe of this man.

"Yes, so far so good. I've made some good new contacts, chatted to a few old friends. I am sure the ceremony will be as boring as always, but what can you do?"

"Not come?" I offered.

He shrugged, drank from his pint and wiped the foam from his top lip with the back of his hand. It made me wonder what it would be like to kiss the beer droplets from there. He had particularly plump and inviting lips.

"I have been informed I have to be here. Means I must be getting another trophy or something."

"It must be nice to be so casual about it," I remarked without thinking. Darren just laughed.

"It must sound like I'm a total bastard. Sorry. I do like getting these things—always good to know I'm doing things right, you know? But once you've been to one of these dos you've been to them all." His northern accent was more prominent when he let down his guard and laughed.

"Sorry, I didn't mean to offend you."

"No, not at all. It's refreshing to be told the truth. I get sick of being pandered to."

"Well, I can pull out some insults too if you'd like, you know, to really make your night."

He laughed again, making my insides churn in a pleasurable way. "I'm okay for now. Save those for after the ceremony—you can bring me back down a peg or two."

I nodded then took a deep draft of my water. The ice coldness chilled me, a momentary relief from the heat burning through my veins.

"Do you want to come and sit at my table?" he asked. "My companion got fed up of me talking business and left with a friend of hers so there's space."

I was supposed to go back to the kitchens to monitor how things were going on behind the scenes, but I was seriously tempted by his offer. Not just because he had enough money to buy himself an island or because he was smoking hot. Oh, who was I trying to kid? He might have been a bit funny but mostly I said yes because I wanted to snog him then get him to part with his cash. Put like that it made me sound like a prostitute, but you know what I mean. I hope. I'd really like him to bring some business my way, or buy me a jet plane or maybe a pony. Frivolous or practical, his cash would make my life easier.

The table he led me to was near the front, just at the edge of the dance floor where a stage had been erected. I made a mental note to praise the staff who had come in early to set up the tables. The white cloth was immaculate and the flowers looked stunning and crisply fresh. Everything was perfect.

"So, what got you into the whole entertainment business, Kerry?" Darren asked when we took our seats.

"My dad owned a pub when I was little. I loved it. I used to long for the day when I could serve behind the bar but he left the trade before I was old enough to. I was a barmaid for years while I put myself through college and university and once I'd gotten the degree I decided to get myself a pub of my own. Then I saw this place quite by accident, fell in love, took out a stonking great loan and the rest is history."

"Sounds like you've got a very sound business head on your shoulders, Kerry."

"I like to think so." I blushed at his compliment. "I've made my fair share of mistakes but they've all worked out in the end."

"That's business." Darren replied. Then the tone of conversation changed dramatically. "I hope you don't mind me saying, but I think you're stunning."

I felt more stunned than stunning. Where had that comment come from? "Well, thank you."

"I know it's a little unprofessional, but I didn't get this far without speaking my mind, you know?"

"Sure," I squeaked. My head felt light and completely devoid of ideas. All the blood in my body seemed equally split between my cheeks and my nether regions. I was embarrassed and turned on—it was a strange combination to say the least.

"When I see something I like, I go for it." His gaze dipped down to my breasts and waist then back up to my face.

"Well…" Finally, my brain rebooted and the words leaped forth. "You'll have to work a bit harder to get me. I'm not easily satisfied."

"Really?" His right eyebrow rose impressively. "I do enjoy a challenge."

Just then the arrival of another entrepreneur changed the focus of the conversation. I was very surprised to find Greg Stamford standing beside me. Especially because the seating plan I'd done had put the two guys far away from each other.

"Hello." I smiled. "Are you at the right table? I thought Akshay Mistry was meant to sit here."

"No, I'm definitely at the right table. Apparently they made a last-minute change." He stopped paying me any attention and looked over to Darren. "Hi, they're playing this game again."

"How unusual, eh?" Darren's Scouse roots came through as he spoke to his biggest business rival. "We shouldn't be talking, it will spoil their illusion."

The gentlemen must have glanced at me long enough to realize I looked confused. Greg pulled up a chair and wafted his sharp, light aftershave in my direction. He continued the conversation and pulled me into it.

"Every time we attend something like this, parties, award ceremonies…"

"Prize givings, charity dos." Darren continued Greg's sentence.

"Any time Darren and I are in the same room, the organisers orchestrate it so we have to share space and so the press can get some photos of us staring daggers at each other."

"It's old hat," Darren agreed, "but it guarantees them space in the tabloids and celeb mags."

"Oh, well. Do you two mind?"

I found myself at the center of two intense stares. I was quite deliciously uncomfortable—it wasn't every day I got scrutinised by two eligible bachelors. I batted my gaze from side to side, almost making myself dizzy while I waited for one of them to speak.

"It's part of the game." Greg responded first with a noncommittal shrug.

"One of these days we'll embrace and kiss just to freak them out." Darren's eyes sparkled with mischief and Greg's dark gaze narrowed reproachfully. I didn't think he appreciated that plan.

"Well, don't let me get in your way." I leaned back in my chair as if to give them room to embrace. The look on their faces was priceless and I laughed as I rocked back to my position. "Only kidding."

A drum roll and a blast of music announced the arrival of the compère and our attention was transferred to the stage. While people clapped for the first nominee I felt a gentle touch on my right arm. I looked around and found Greg's handsome face far closer to me than I had expected it to be. The rest of his delicious body was curved in toward me too.

He leaned in farther and I directed my ear near to his lips. I tried not to think of how it would feel to have his lips and teeth nibble on my earlobe. I failed miserably.

"You're the owner here, aren't you?" he asked.

I nodded. The crowd were quiet, so were obviously expecting an announcement. I didn't want to disturb the moment.

"Yes, Kerry Matthews, nice to meet you." I glanced his way and saw him smile, the hard lines of his face softening a little, making him seem more approachable. He leaned in to talk again so I tipped my head once more so I could hear him.

"Great place you've got here."

I turned to thank him and he was still really close to my face. Our lips were centimetres away from meeting. I pulled back a little. He didn't move at all.

"Thanks." I smiled, uncomfortable at his close proximity. Not because I didn't want him near—I suspected we'd have a lot of fun getting up close and naked. No, I felt on edge because I barely knew the guy yet he was arrogantly invading my personal space. It unsettled me.

"I'm hosting a launch party and I'm looking for somewhere special to hold it."

I shifted position. If I couldn't see how close he was I couldn't be disturbed. That was what I thought, but it wasn't true. I could sense him there, feel his breath on my cheek and all kinds of flirty and filthy images crowded my mind. I fought through them to concentrate on his words.

"I'd love to use Diamonds. It would be perfect."

"Brilliant." I nodded and faced him again. He was still uncomfortably close. "We'll talk afterwards. I can give you prices and dates."

"Thank you." His face really was changed by a smile. I wondered how many people he had charmed into agreeing with him just by beaming at them. I was sure it would be a considerable number. A strong hand on my thigh broke my concentration. I still looked at Greg. He still grinned but he also squeezed my leg quite forcefully.

I wasn't sure how long my jaw hung limply open but when I realized I clamped it back shut. I wondered if he was just a touchy kind of person, then dismissed that idea completely. Greg looked far too stern. Yet his hand was lying on my upper thigh. I gulped as he squeezed again. I didn't know what to do. I should have pulled away—his touch was rather inappropriate considering we'd only just been introduced. I didn't want to remove his hand from my body, though, it felt good. I also didn't want to offend a man who was clearly interested in hiring out the club.

He didn't move his hand. He didn't squeeze or stroke, he just left it there imprinted on my thigh. I could feel it burning through my skirt to my skin. His fingertips rested just below the hem, they were on my naked flesh and I imagined Greg insinuating them underneath my dress and up past my drenched knickers to my pussy.

I sat still, like a statue. I looked up at the stage but I didn't take in any of what was happening. I wondered if Greg's hand on my body was the blatant signal indicating he wanted to fuck me that I thought it was. A few moments later, my mind still reeling with what might happen next, I was surprised to feel Darren's hand slide onto my left thigh.

I looked over toward his unruly red hair and gazed at his pretty blue eyes. I was sure shock was written all over my face. He just winked. I smiled weakly. I wasn't sure what else to do.

Two hot guys who coincidentally possessed enough money between them to buy my bar and all the other shops and houses in the immediate area were feeling me up at the same time. I found myself in a quandary. How the hell was I going to keep them both satisfied? There was only one of me but there were two of them. I supposed they could share me, but would they want to? It was a kinky idea, one that really, really appealed to me, but they were bitter rivals. I was positive they wouldn't want to crawl into bed with each other and definitely not just to be with me.

Maybe I was getting ahead of myself, but I certainly didn't want to do anything to offend either billionaire. It was mind-boggling that both of them were showing me interest. I sat still and tried not to breathe. I was afraid it was all going to go terribly wrong.

"...Greg Stamford!" The compère—Dave something I think his name was—looked at our table. The spotlight was fixed on us and Greg stood up, removed his hand from my thigh and strode toward the stage.

"After this, would you like to join me for a nightcap?" Darren didn't waste any time, immediately turning to proposition me.

"Well, I have to stay here until the end," I replied, "I still have work to do."

Darren nodded and waited, pinning me under his ice-blue gaze.

"If you wait, I might be free then."

"Okay, I'll wait. You'll be worth it."

I was flattered. I know, awfully non-PC of me, but a hot billionaire wanting to spend time with me turned my head. I wasn't used to it. I didn't get many propositions at work, at least not from people who weren't drunk or married or unattractive. I was on cloud nine. Then Greg came back with an award in hand.

"So, after we've finished here do you want to come to my room and talk business and maybe more?"

Billionaires are so to the point. Well, at least these ones were.

"Actually, *mate*"—Darren spat the word, making it sound less than friendly—"I've just arranged to have a nightcap with the lady."

"Oh, you did, did you? Well, I got there first."

"Fast isn't always good, Greg," Darren snapped back.

"You only say that because Stamford's get the apps out there first." Greg looked cocky. Darren looked like he was about to explode. I felt like piggy in the middle.

"Full of bugs and glitches."

"Nothing that can't be fixed." Greg seemed mostly unruffled.

"Well, this can't be fixed. Kerry has agreed to come with me after the show."

"We have to talk business, I'm going to host a launch party here. Kerry already told me we'd talk after the ceremony." Greg's voice was raising with each comment. Soon everyone would hear and the ceremony would be ruined by two hard-headed big shots. I'd be a laughingstock.

"Well, you two talk. I'll wait until you're finished and then wake her up for a nightcap."

"You little —"

"Would you two stop it?" I whispered. "Have you never learnt how to share nicely? There is plenty of me to go round."

Both boys stopped and appraised my curves. My blood turned to fire inside me. I felt like I was trapped in an inferno between their gazes.

"Would you like that?" Darren whispered, looking to Greg.

"I would like you both to stop shouting and acting like kids," I snapped.

"But would you like to spend the night with Greg and me, together? The three of us?"

I looked left. Greg was looking stoic. I didn't think he let his emotions show very often. I looked right and Darren was staring intently at me.

"Yes, yes, I would." What else could I say? I couldn't run the risk of upsetting either of these men, and I did want to spend more time with them both, and who was I to turn down a threesome with the most handsome men in the room?

"What do you say, Greg?" Darren asked, "Share nicely, just for tonight?"

I melted into the background as the two enemies faced off. I could almost hear the wheels in Greg's mind turning, evaluating the pros and cons while Darren's icy stare spurred him on.

"Okay, just this once," Greg conceded, "but no funny business."

"No funny business." Darren nodded and held out his hand. Greg clasped it briefly. I felt like I'd just been bought at a slave market and it felt surprisingly good. I had brought peace to two warring factions, temporarily at least. I wondered if I could keep up with both of them?

Chapter Two

"Are you finished?" Darren appeared at my elbow the moment the crowds of people thinned.

"I believe so," I replied. "I've taken loads of bookings."

"Good, you've got my birthday booked in, right?"

"Yes." I nodded. "It's all in the book."

Just then Greg arrived. Both boys still appeared immaculate in their suits. I felt a little frazzled around the edges. My head throbbed in time with my feet and my skin prickled with moisture. It had been a long and busy night—profitable, though, financially and, if I played my cards right, sexually too.

"So, are you two ready?" he asked. "I'll get Chester to bring the limo round."

"We can go in mine," Darren snapped.

"Oh, don't start this again." I shook my head. "Decide nicely or I'll be getting the damn Tube home."

If the billionaires could be so abrupt with me, I'd be snappy with them.

"Fine," Darren shrugged, "but we're going back to my hotel."

"Where are you staying?"

While the boys argued amongst themselves I took the date book and locked it away in my desk. I'd filled up a lot of the year and some dates had drifted into the next one. With the business I'd secured I was guaranteed to finish the fiscal year pleasantly in profit. I might even be able to afford a holiday. If I could persuade myself to stay away from Diamonds long enough.

When I walked back over to them the boys were silent.

"So, are we actually ready now?"

Greg reacted first, slipping his arm into mine and smiling.

"Yes, it seems me and Darren are staying at the same hotel."

"Wonderful." I smiled, intensely relieved. "Lead the way."

Darren took hold of my other arm and we strode out together. I wasn't expecting the barrage of flashing lights and yelled questions that greeted us. I supposed I had been a little naïve. The boys, with the aid of some huge security guards, pushed past the demands and we scooted into the back of a shiny black limousine. The mellow scent of leather filled the interior. Everything sparkled. I felt like we were in a separate car to the driver who was way, way down at the front.

"Are we going to the hotel, sir?" a polite voice asked. It sounded like it came from behind me, which was puzzling until I realized there was some kind of intercom device. Greg reached to the side of the limo and pressed a button.

"Yes, please, Chester."

I would have liked more space to actually enjoy the ride home but I was crowded by two competing men and so spent my time flipping my gaze from one to the other, answering questions. Both were squeezed up close to me and both seemed determined to seduce me. I found that mind-spinningly crazy.

"What perfume are you wearing?" Darren ducked his head to sniff at my neck. I was very aware of his lips hovering just above my pulse point. I wished he'd kiss me there.

"Oh, I don't know. Something fruity." My mind went completely blank.

"You smell good enough to eat." Darren continued and his lips did touch my skin but only for the briefest second. My whole body tightened at the gentle kiss.

"Your dress is beautiful." It seemed Greg was not to be outdone—in fact he boldly ran his hand down my body from my shoulder, over my breast and lower. "I love the feel of velvet."

"Thank you," I squeaked then cleared my throat. "Thanks, I love velvet too."

Tension zinged through me, sexual and otherwise. These two guys who I'd only just met were making me into a battlefield. They were warring to control me.

I wasn't a woman who enjoyed being mollycoddled. I took decisions, I dove into situations and I expected all of my staff to be respectful to both men and women. I'd reprimanded several for sexism and would go as far as to sack someone if they didn't change their ways. I should have been appalled by the situation—I wasn't just a trophy or a business contract. I should have kicked up a fuss and left then and there.

But I didn't. I liked being the center of attention. I liked being the prize they both wanted.

I waited for the next move but we pulled up outside the hotel so I had to wait until we exited the car. Again, both men linked arms with me. It was cold outside but apart from the cool breeze on my cheeks I barely felt it because their hard bodies protected me from the elements.

They whisked me across the marble frontage, past the liveried doorman and into a huge reception area. It glittered with prestige and marble. Everything was perfect, neat and tidy. There was nothing overly ornate or showy but you could tell by the purposeful minimalism that this was a very classy place. The kind of place I'd only ever imagined visiting.

We moved across the hall into the bar. Again it was big, shiny but understated. The bar was long and all the staff behind it were in immaculately cut uniforms. They all looked smart and tidy and I looked on with envy. I wished I could get my own staff to look so impressive.

"What would you like to drink?" Darren asked and smirked at Greg.

"I'd love a glass of water, really," I replied, "I'm so thirsty."

"I'll get them to send over some water too, but should we have some champagne? It was a very good night for us all after all."

Both Darren and Greg had won awards and I was sure they'd both made several deals too as they played the room.

"Yes, why not?" Greg answered before me. "Champagne sounds good."

When Darren moved away Greg turned to me.

"Look, Kerry, I really would love to spend the night with you but it is killing me to be nice to him."

"This is you being nice?"

"Exactly." He almost smiled. I found it surprisingly endearing. "Please can we dump the other guy?"

"No." I was very firm, it surprised even me. "No, I said I wanted to spend time with you both, so that is what's going to happen. If you don't like it, you can leave."

"God, woman. You're infuriatingly stubborn." He growled.

"Now that is a case of the pot calling the kettle black." I laughed.

Greg sighed. "I'm not used to being told what to do, Kerry. I'm the one in control."

"I'd noticed, but if you want me, you play by my rules." It was fun playing him at his own game.

"Oh, I want you." His growl turned to a gravelly purr. It wasn't cute, it was the noise of a killer beast merely at rest. Any moment he could pounce and rip me apart. It turned me on. I wriggled in my seat and my damp knickers chafed against my plump lips.

"Then you'll share nicely." I leaned in and kissed him. He was shocked, almost as much as I was. His lips were hard and ungiving for a moment—I thought maybe I'd pushed him too far—but then they melted, opened and pushed back and I felt his pent-up arousal running into me. I released my frustrated desire with every move of my lips.

We pulled apart and I had to pant to regain my breath while he licked his lips like he was savoring the taste.

"I'll do it for you," he said. I was intoxicated with the power of having him under my control.

"Hey, I want one too." Darren came back, placed a glass of water before me and pressed his lips to mine. His were plump and giving. He prodded his tongue between my lips, into my mouth, taking control of the kiss and control of me. I felt like I might explode into a million pieces. I hadn't been kissed in months and now I'd had two smoking hot smooches in as many minutes from two very hot but very different men.

"Okay," I gasped when he pulled away, "now you're even."

The guys glowered at each other. I looked around the room to calm my nerves. Not a single person looked at us. Obviously such things happened often in bars of high-class hotels. It didn't happen often to me. At all, in fact. I wondered if I was dreaming. I pinched my thigh below the table. It hurt. I definitely wasn't dreaming.

A tall, skinny waiter brought us a bottle of champagne stood in a silver ice bucket. Balanced on his tray were three tall flutes. He transferred everything to our table with great pomp. I was in awe of his skill.

"Thank you," I called. He nodded politely and walked off.

I knew a little about wine and champagne, only because my barman told me what I needed to order. The champagne in the bucket was clearly expensive — I'd never even heard of the name — and it was suitably French, obviously. I was sure Darren had ordered the most expensive in the place just to outdo Greg. I outdid both of them by just sipping at my water.

"Shall we take the rest of the bottle to my room?"

I nearly choked when I heard what Greg had said.

"Pardon?"

"Well, you wanted us to share nicely and I don't think that even in an establishment like this where confidentiality is taken seriously we could share you, nicely or otherwise, right here in the bar."

It took a moment to register that Greg Stamford, billionaire high-flyer and serious hottie, was propositioning me for a threesome. I'd agreed to it earlier, but it still seemed too much like a fairy tale to be actually real.

"I agree, mate. We'd get chucked out. Want to go to my room? It's the Ambassador Suite." Darren announced this like I should be impressed. Maybe it was the most expensive room in the hotel? I wasn't sure.

"My room has the best view over the city," Greg snapped.

"Yes, that's what they tell people who can't get in the Ambassador Suite."

"Boys, stop it." My voice was quite loud. The low murmur of conversation stopped for a moment, then carried on.

"Look. You are both very rich, I get it. You both want to be top dog, I get that too, but would you stop bickering like bloody schoolboys, okay? I am very flattered, truly, and I never in a million years would have imagined being in this situation..." I left the sentence hanging and gathered my thoughts.

"Please don't say no." Darren's smile dissipated. "I'm sorry."

"Well..." I tried to continue with my tirade. I had the moral high ground. I was going to say thanks but no thanks and leave both gentleman hanging, but say that I hoped they'd both still honor their bookings. I was going to make a stand, I really was. Then... Well, I'm not quite sure what happened.

"I'm sorry too," Greg added. "We're just billionaires used to getting our own way. Let's go to the Ambassador Suite — it's a lovely room."

Had I heard that right? Had Greg Stamford apologized and ceded to his most hated rival?

"Yes, let's." Darren nodded. "Please, Kerry?"

I challenge any woman alive to not cave in when hit with not one but two sets of puppy dog eyes from intensely handsome men. I couldn't do it.

"Come on then," I whispered, "lead the way."

Darren beckoned a waiter and pointed at the bottle and glasses. No words were spoken but the waiter seemed to know exactly what was needed from him.

The lift was large, gold and sparkly. I was in awe of that, which I thought didn't bode well since I'd not even reached the heart of the hotel. It was huge too but it felt like it was crowded with dozens of bodies because Darren and Greg squashed up close to me. I could barely catch my breath, I was completely overwhelmed. Darren grabbed my left hand and Greg punched the number into the plate. Obviously he'd stayed in the Ambassador Suite before.

When Greg noticed my fingers were entwined with his rival's, he took my other hand. It was at once comforting and scary to have these two men fighting for possession over my body. I felt like I was in good hands with these two strapping guys but I was also nervous about how they might pull me apart when they both decided to maul me.

That vision sounded unpleasant but it wasn't really. As long as no one came to blows and we all ended up satisfied, I could see it being a rather pleasant experience, but the nerves still rattled in the bottom of my tummy like that one last coin you can't get out of a piggy bank. What if it all went wrong? My proportions weren't those of a supermodel, I had a stomach and it wobbled. My boobs were quite perky but they were real and so they sagged into my body when not held up by my bra. These little imperfections niggled at me because, although I was fairly happy in my own skin, I was pretty unhappy with revealing it to others.

Sticks and stones may break my bones but words will never hurt me? Well, that's a pile of crap, I can tell you. Years of fat jibes from school to university and beyond had made me self-conscious. I had never really been fat either, just tall and well proportioned before the rest of my class. At ten I had been five foot five and an adult size twelve. My body mass index had been perfect but I was still called all the fat names under the sun. It had hurt even though I knew they were wrong.

And when I stopped worrying about my body I worried about being with these particular two guys. It wasn't that they scared me — they were both charming, handsome and sweet. But like owning a domesticated lion, you felt safe having it around but you never knew when it might turn savage.

The motion of the lift was barely perceptible, a slight hum accompanied by a sinking feeling in my stomach, like someone squishing it down to fit more inside. Darren snuggled even closer to me and nibbled on my earlobe.

Greg, not to be outdone, slid his hand over my waist and up to cup my breast and at the same time he dipped his head and cradled his lips in the dip between my neck and my shoulder. Just the barest movement vibrated through me, sending shivers of need down to nestle between my thighs.

Ear, neck, breast, hand. I was surrounded by manliness. I was completely clothed but felt stripped bare. What if someone got in now and saw me like this? Would they presume me a prostitute — would they even care? It seemed you could get away with murder if you were rich.

I didn't find out. When the doors opened, the guys led me onto their floor and there wasn't another person in sight. It was obvious this was where the top-class rooms were because there were only a few doors dotted down the bright cream corridor, which was adorned with muted peach marble columns and the occasional picture in a gold gilt frame.

"Just here," Darren said removing a card from his inside jacket pocket and confidently stroking it through the slot. He beckoned me forward and I walked in. The lights came on automatically and I gasped in wonder. I really didn't want to, I'd been going to act cool, but the room was so big and so opulent—and it was only a sitting area. I could see an archway to the left, which I imagined led to the bedroom and bathroom, and God alone knew how big they'd be!

There wasn't much time to take in the details because the door shut and seconds later I was squashed quite pleasantly between two hard bodies. Greg claimed my lips and Darren nibbled my neck. I wasn't sure who unzipped my dress but both sets of hands pushed it down.

My brain didn't engage, I just did. I knew this was the opportunity of a lifetime. I was in the middle of a dream come true, a very erotic dream, in fact. I had imagined what it would be like to fuck two guys at once, I suspected most women had. It was the attraction of that potent desire that sparked from two separate men bathing you with appreciation and lust. I didn't even think to protest. I didn't want to. I simply focused on the moment. I was eaten up with desire and all I wanted was to get Darren and Greg out of their clothes and into me.

I was naked in a matter of minutes but it took me a lot longer to get rid of their clothes, or at least it seemed that way. They kept distracting me with kisses and nibbles and caresses.

While I concentrated on removing Greg's burgundy tie, Darren traced kisses down my spine. I shivered, then moaned and before I could pull open all his shirt buttons Greg was dipping into my cleavage, cupping my flesh, brushing his lips over my skin, making me tingle all over.

I lost track of who was where and I just grabbed blindly at items of clothing when they came near. I could hardly coordinate myself. Kisses all over me dampened my senses and set my knees wobbling.

"Bedroom." Darren spoke one word and I found myself led off, Darren to the left of me wearing his trousers but with his shirt unbuttoned. He was surprisingly buff beneath his suit, his shoulders broad, his stomach tight. Greg was to the right, and only the top few buttons of his pale blue shirt were unbuttoned, but I saw a promising triangle of sun-bronzed skin covered with a spattering of dark hairs.

I was sandwiched by two of the hottest and most eligible bachelors in the whole entire world. That took a little digesting, but the real miracle was that they were sharing me and nicely at that.

The bedroom was huge and the bed in it palatial. I swear I crawled half a mile to reach the middle of it— it felt like that anyway. I was very aware of my breasts and butt wiggling as the guys stood either side of the huge, springy divan divesting themselves of what clothing still clung to them.

The hair on Greg's chest extended down in a tornado-shaped trail to his belly button and lower. I loved the mess of dark curls nestled above his cock. I didn't look for too long because I had two men to visually masticate so only took a whistle-stop tour of their bodies.

Darren's body was hairless, his skin summer-cloud white, which wasn't a surprise because his sun-colored hair suggested he would be pale and interesting and he was indeed. Both cocks were hard, similar in proportions with Darren's being a tad thicker and Greg's a little longer with a subtle crick that pointed it slightly to the left.

I had knots in my stomach. I doubted they'd ever untangle. I felt heavy with need and anticipation. What would they do to me? It was a question that could only be answered practically.

Not a word was spoken. Both guys joined me on the bed. Darren scrambled over eagerly and Greg sat then rolled in a far more sedate fashion until he was up against me, his dick pressed into my thigh and his hand on my breast. Darren copied the pose on the other side and I rocked and rolled my hips in the middle while the different hands molded and tickled my chest. Greg's hands were bigger, rougher than Darren's. Both delighted me.

Greg slipped his fingers down over my ribs and trailed over my stomach. I held my breath as he took in the curve, loving his touch but worried about his reaction to the area of my body that caused most consternation.

He moaned. The warm air of his breath tickled my ear and I felt the lust rolling around his chest. Skimming through my pubic hair, he purposefully sought out my clit, nestled between my lips and eager for touch. I gasped and dug my head back into the pillows each time he gently rubbed against the little protuberance of flesh. It amazed me how much pleasure was stored there and how it whizzed around my whole body in such a short amount of time.

Darren trailed his touch downwards, settled his hand between my thighs and dipped his fingers inside me, stretching and filling me with ease. I was so wet and so ecstatic as the men did what they could to manually pleasure me. I curled and stretched to the strains of desire and turned to face Greg. Darren's wet fingers trailed over my hip and cupped my buttock while I writhed against his rival. Greg's fingers still manipulated my clit and I teetered on the brink of ecstasy. He curved to face me, meeting me lip to lip, his kiss undulating at the same speed as his digits, rolling ecstasy through me, connecting a line direct from my lips to my clit.

I wanted to feel more of him, more of both of them. Darren stroked my back and buttocks and I was overtaken with the urge to please them both. I wiggled lower and dropped my kisses down Greg's gently prickling chin to his neck and collarbone. I kept shifting lower, kissing down Greg's lightly furred chest and to his stomach.

Aggressively I pushed him down onto his back and pulled up onto my knees. Darren moved and adapted as I leaned over and gently licked along Greg's hot length. I enjoyed the feel of him against my tongue and lips and wondered about the crackling noise behind me. A moment later it was apparent that Darren had sheathed himself with a condom. I could feel the familiar plastic-like chill of it when it slipped between my raised buttocks. I stuck my bottom out and encouraged him to push inside me—I wanted to be filled.

Everything warmed up soon enough. I stretched to accommodate the width of his dick and continued to lick and tease Greg's cock until his hips bumped up and down in frustration and finally I let him sink in between my lips. Two cocks and me, the perfect equation. I was full, aching and wantonly sexual. I felt sexier than I ever had before. I commanded the desire of two powerful men and they were both determinedly using me for their pleasure. I loved it.

Greg entwined his fingers in my hair. I took more of him between my lips. He was long and so it was a struggle to take him fully into my mouth. I twisted and turned my head and used my tongue to lap at the sensitive dip under his cock head. It seemed to work. I could taste his emissions, salty and mellow, and eagerly continued the blow job.

My concentration wandered as Darren upped the tempo. I released Greg's dick from my mouth and leaned my head on his thigh while Darren rammed harder and deeper into me. I curled my hand around Greg's wet erection and hung on for dear life until Darren came with a grunt of satisfaction.

"I need you," Greg gasped. "Please let me fuck you." I looked up with a gentle smile on my lips. I liked the way he had asked me, it seemed almost old-fashioned and quaint, though the situation was neither.

"Pass me a condom, please." I turned to Darren who'd collapsed on the bed beside me, chest heaving, flaccid cock slipping from its confines. He nodded, extended his arm lazily and knocked a packet from the bedside table into his fist. He passed it to me and I transferred my attention to Greg. I ripped open the packet at speed but as carefully as I could manage. I placed the condom over the tip of him and rolled it down to snugly coat his erection. I split my thighs around him and hovered over his cock. He maneuvered himself until the tip of his dick slipped in and I sank down until he filled me.

It was at once the same as and completely different to fucking Darren. Greg's cock rubbed and slid where Darren's stretched me wide. I was more in control in my position on top of Greg. I moved at the speed I desired and felt him humping his hips up to create more friction. I glimpsed down and locked stares with him. He was so mysterious—even in the middle of the fuck he seemed guarded, though I could see his lust and enjoyment painted across his cheeks in russet red and in the deep, dark depths of his black, expanded pupils.

My eyelids fluttered shut. Greg sought out my clit with his thick finger. I was grateful for his attention and desperate for my own release. I climbed toward total ecstasy and felt another hand on my body. Darren slapped my bottom and squeezed it as I rode to my soul-deep satisfaction.

Greg came moments after me. I felt his cock spasm inside me, in time with my clenching walls. Darren's hand fell from my buttock and I slipped off Greg's hard body to snuggle between the two men.

I knew then that it was the start of something amazing but I didn't realize just what until much later.

Chapter Three

Darren insisted I went home in his limo, which was a surreal experience. I didn't feel right in such a big interior all on my own—I didn't feel like I deserved it. I had two billionaires' contact details in my handbag and felt like I glowed with sexual satisfaction.

It wasn't until the next day that I really thought about what had happened. It had been a brilliant experience and I wouldn't have changed it for the world but I was worried about the follow-up. They had given me their numbers and I had given them mine. Should I wait for them to ring me or should I ring them? Also, who should I talk to first? Would it get back to the other and make him jealous? I had always been inclined to ask far more questions than I should. I was a woman of action but I was also a woman of crippling scrutiny. I never made a move until I'd thought out several possible outcomes first.

I was stopped mid-fluster by my mobile ringing. I answered it without thought. It was Greg.

"Hi, Kerry."

"Oh, hiya, Greg." I dropped the tea towel in my hand and bent to pick it up. Every other person in the kitchen suddenly went quiet. I walked toward my office. I didn't want the workforce to listen in on the call in case it got personal.

"I just wanted you to know I really enjoyed last night."

"Yes, so did I." I rushed out of the kitchen and down the corridor to my office. I shut the door behind me.

"Especially the late night part. I'd love to see you again and soon but I'm mid-flight to New York. I'm going to be away for a week or so."

"Oh, okay." I sat down heavily on my chair. "Thanks for letting me know."

"I didn't want you to think I wasn't interested. Has *he* rung you yet?"

"If you mean Darren, no, not yet."

The noise that echoed down the phone was the epitome of pointed indifference mixed with an edge of pride.

"Just be careful around him, Kerry. He's a complete twat, but he's a dangerous twat at that."

The word sounded strange in his cut-glass accent.

"Well, you would say that," I replied. "I'm a big girl, you know."

"You're very capable, I know," he replied with a suggestive purr. I covered my blushing cheeks with my hand even though he couldn't see me. "I just don't want you to get hurt. When I'm back in the UK I'll ring you, we'll go out."

"Oh, we will, will we?" I bristled at his presumptuousness.

"If you want to." There was a waver of doubt to his tone and it made him sound vulnerable. I found it infinitely appealing. "You do want to, don't you?"

"Yes, I do." I put him out of his misery. "But I'm not going to be at your beck and call, you know? I have my own life to run, Mr Stamford, my own schedule. Don't expect me to jump at your bidding."

"Oh, darling, if I'm commanding you to do something it's going to be far more exciting than merely jumping, trust me." The suggestive growl was back. I clenched my thighs together as lewd images rushed through my mind.

"Well, that's good to know," I responded, "but I have to get back to work. We open in an hour and there's still loads to do."

"I'll ring you again soon, Kerry. Bye."

I'd just gotten myself composed and back out in the club when my phone rang again. It was Darren.

"What are you doing tomorrow?" he asked, without a greeting.

"Well, hello, Darren," I said with a shake of my head. What was it with these guys? They didn't own me just because I'd slept with them.

"Hi, what are you doing tomorrow?" He repeated his question.

"I'm working."

"All day?"

"Pretty much."

"Oh. I wanted to take you out."

"Well, I'm busy. I do have a club to run, you know."

"I know you do. When is your next day off?"

I smiled. I didn't do days off as a general rule but my second-in-command was always moaning at me for working too much. I could leave him in charge for one day, it'd make him happy.

"Wednesday, but I was planning to wash my hair—"

Darren chuckled. The rumble rolled around in my stomach and directed my thoughts to my crotch area once more. "I'll wash your hair for you. I'll pick you up around midday, okay?"

"I suppose so." I grinned.

"Good, I can't wait. I had lots of fun last night." His tone softened.

"So did I, but I have to work now. See you, Darren."

"Bye, Kerry."

I struggled to control my leaping heart and spinning stomach. What the hell was I going to wear, and moreover, what were we going to do? Darren hadn't told me. I was fairly sure we'd not be talking business but apart from that I had no clue. Two billionaires—handsome, hot control freaks. How would we cope with each other? I wasn't sure but I knew it'd be fun to find out.

* * * *

"I'll buy it," I snapped. "I do have my own money, you know." I crossed my arms and pouted.

"But I said today was my treat," Darren replied. "So I'm paying."

"Look," I sighed. "I am very happy to be out with you, in fact I'll even let you buy dinner if that makes you happy, but I am my own woman. I don't need you to pay for every little thing I want." Of all the things I'd ever expected to be annoyed by, having things bought for me hadn't been one of them, but this shopping trip with Darren was getting repetitive. I'd pick something up, say I would purchase it, he'd insist he'd buy it then I'd storm out of the shop without it. I wasn't going to let any man buy his way into my affections.

The cute purse in the quaint little boutique went the same way. I slammed it down on the pay desk and stalked out. I was incensed. I knew it might seem a little crazy, but I had always paid my own way in the world, fought to make my business a success so I could afford all I wanted.

Darren caught up with me as I stormed off.

"Kerry, look, I'm sorry," he pleaded, grabbing my arm. "Don't be mad at me, I just want to treat you well. I want to buy you pretty things to make you happy."

I couldn't look into his sincere blue eyes without feeling a tug of remorse.

"Look, Darren, I mean no offense, but I'm my own woman, you know?"

He nodded.

"I don't mind you offering to buy me something, but you don't need to buy *everything*. It makes me uncomfortable, makes me feel like I'm scrounging off you."

"But you're not. I have the money and I can't think of a better way to spend it than on a beautiful lady."

"Flatterer." I slapped his arm. He just shrugged and smiled. "All right, then, I tell you what. I'll let you buy me something but then if I want to get something for myself you won't insist on paying for it, all right?"

Darren nodded once more.

"Good, now where do you want to take me?"

I was whisked down past Harrods and deeper into the exclusive shopping heart of Knightsbridge until we reached a very posh and frankly scary-looking shop.

"Darren, I don't know if they'll have anything—"

"Oh, trust me, they will." He smiled.

Hesitantly, I followed him in. If the models in the window were anything to go by I'd not get my left pinkie into any of the lingerie within, let alone the rest of my body.

"Good afternoon, Margaret." Darren greeted the shop owner with warmth in his gaze. "My friend is looking for a corset and matching items, what do you suggest?"

I came under the probing gaze of the stern-looking older woman. My curves were assessed in short shrift.

"Yes, I think she'd look good in the new style that's just come in. Red, dark and sumptuous." She walked out from behind her counter and over to one of the sparse displays. She pulled out a hanger and passed it to Darren.

"Looks good. She'll need to try it on," he said turning the corset in his hands.

Margaret nodded toward the cubicle at the back of the store. "Let me get the matching knickers and a nice pair of stockings for you to try on too." She strode confidently to her stock and pulled out a few items. I didn't think she looked at any labels before passing them over to Darren. "I'm out here if you need any help or a second opinion."

"Thanks, Margaret." Darren grabbed my hand and pulled me toward the changing room. It was a large cubicle, the walls covered in sumptuous gold fabric. I felt like I'd entered a harem. A classy, scroll-framed mirror stood in one corner and a seat was placed diagonally opposite it. Darren sat down.

"You'll have to take all your clothes off," he said with a smirk, "to try these on properly."

"Oh, I will, will I?" I shook my head teasingly. "Dirty old perv."

"Less of the old," he crowed. "Now get your clothes off. I can't wait to see you in this."

Funnily, I didn't even think to disobey his command, because I wanted to do it. Teasing Darren with my nakedness in semi-public thrilled me.

Eagerly I pulled off my T-shirt and my shoes and jeans followed suit. My cheeks filled with heat as I stood before him in just my underwear but his appreciative nod urged me on. I could feel the lust building in him, I could see it in how tensely he sat in the chair.

I removed my bra, slipping the straps from my shoulders at the same time that I unfastened the back latch. I felt the cool air on my skin as I rolled down my knickers. I was completely naked with nothing more than a curtain or two separating me from a very public shop.

"Stunning," he gasped.

"I've not put it on yet," I giggled, wiggling from side to side and sliding my hands across my body to shield it.

"I know." He stood and whisked me into his arms to kiss me. I was very aware of our surroundings at first but soon I melted into the passion of his kiss. He could have fucked me right then and there and I would have let him but he pulled back and let out a shuddering breath.

"The corset," he said and turned to pull it down from its hanger. He worked diligently with competent fingers to press me into the garment and fasten it. I was stunned at how well it fitted. I hadn't told Margaret my size, she'd only looked at me. I also wondered how many other women Darren had cinched into such garments — he certainly seemed well practiced at it.

"Stunning." He stood back and admired me. My breasts stood up proud and boiled over the top of the soft silk that covered my waist and pulled attention to my ample hips. I gripped my fingers around my waist, amazed by how slim it seemed. The garment held me in tightly but not uncomfortably. I could get used to wearing it, I was sure.

Once again Darren pushed himself up against me. His mouth ravaged mine and his hands ran freely up and down my body. I responded with gusto at first. I felt sexy and was incredibly turned on but when I felt the silken wall behind me and I realized where we were I stiffened in fear. I heard voices in the shop. Relief swept through me. Margaret would be distracted for a while serving them and wouldn't be listening to us.

Darren pulled me back toward the armless chair. He sat back on it, opening his trousers to reveal a naked and eager cock beneath. My eyes widened and I started to shake my head, but the lust in his eyes tallied up with that which pulled in the bottom of my stomach and I walked toward him.

He freed a condom from his pocket—the man was well prepared—and sheathed himself. He spun me round and pulled me down into his lap, my back to him. I hovered just above him. He maneuvered his erection until it pressed at my wet entrance. Nothing but a kiss and I was already soaked wet and eager for him.

I slid down over his thick manhood with little problem. I sat still for a moment. He wrapped his arms around me and stroked at the exposed areas of my breasts as I started to move up and down. All the time I was alert to noises outside the changing area. The voices were still mumbling, I couldn't tell what was being said, they were too far away and I was distracted by the harsh panting of Darren's breath merging with mine.

While I rode him he followed the contour of my waist and lower with his fingers until they dipped between my thighs and found my clit. I whimpered and bit my lip. Orgasmic pleasure coursed through my veins. At any moment we could be caught. I couldn't scream or moan, I had to stay quiet. It was torture. I wanted to be noisy, to roar out my pleasure, but I couldn't or we'd be discovered.

I came sharply, my teeth clamped into my lower lip painfully holding in the shout of delight that so wanted to echo around the silken confines of the little room. He shook and stilled moments later, his face pushed up against the line where the fabric met my flesh. When we pulled apart I could see the red line imprint that the force of our coupling had left.

"We better hurry," he whispered. "Margaret will be suspicious."

He helped me unfasten the garment after freeing the condom from his cock and making himself presentable once more. When he unlaced me he started talking again but in a louder tone.

"Yes, that looks lovely, we'll have these."

"Okay," I replied, then whispered the rest. "But I didn't try them all on."

He shrugged and I pulled on my underwear. "They'll fit perfectly, Margaret has a good eye."

He was right, Margaret did have a good eye. She'd picked out the perfect corset for me at a glance. I didn't imagine some knickers and stockings would stump her. Soon enough I was dressed and out in the stark brightness of the shop. Margaret's other customers had left and she was behind the till, beaming.

"Were they all right for you then?" she asked, politely.

"Fitted perfectly," I declared, trying hard not to look embarrassed. My cheeks heated anyway but I tried not to look down guiltily. I met her stare.

"Absolutely spot on," Darren added. "Thank you, Margaret."

"My pleasure," she replied, taking the proffered credit card from Darren's hand. As the transaction worked she wrapped my purchases in tissue. I just wanted out of the shop. Could she smell the sex on us? Did we look rumpled and sexually replete? A lady who could pick out a corset for a woman at first glance would obviously be able to spot the signs of a couple who'd had nookie in her changing room. I squirmed from foot to foot, uncomfortably aware of my damp underwear and the warm tingle left over from my recent orgasm.

"I hope you continue to enjoy your purchases." Margaret passed the bag to Darren. "Thanks for visiting."

"Always a pleasure," Darren replied with a wink. "Goodbye, Margaret."

"Do you think she knew what we were up to?" I asked Darren when we were farther down the street. He shrugged.

"If she did, she didn't care."

"You are a bad influence on me." I shook my head and groaned. "I've just had sex in a fancy boutique!"

"So did I," he sang, "and it was glorious."

The rest of the shopping trip was less eventful. We finished with a lovely meal and he left me at my front door with a kiss and several bags filled with goodies. He'd gotten his way and had thoroughly spoiled me all day.

"I'd love to stay," he said after the last kiss on my doorstep, "but I have to fly to Milan in two hours' time."

"Okay." I nodded. "Well, ring me when you're back in town."

"Oh, I will." He smiled. "Depend on it."

Chapter Four

"I'm back," Greg declared. "Did you miss me?"

"Who are you?" I teased him through the phone while I stretched my body. I'd not been awake long. I'd been at the club until the early hours the night before. I was always there late on a Saturday night. I slept in on a Sunday. I looked at the bedside clock — it was just after noon.

"Oh, ha ha. I've not been away that long. Can I see you today?"

"Today?" I sat up. "Mmm, maybe. I've only just woken up and I have to be at the club tonight."

"Can't you have the night off? I was hoping to take you somewhere special."

"It's a bit short notice, Greg." I sighed. I wasn't going to tell him I'd already agreed to let Taylor watch the club that night anyway. He was coping well and I really did need to spend more time relaxing and less time at work. "Can't we do it another night?"

"No, it has to be tonight. Please, Kerry? I'm desperate to see you."

"Really?" I twisted a curl around my finger and giggled coquettishly. I couldn't believe how young this man made me feel.

"Really," he insisted. "I couldn't get you out of my mind. I need to see you."

"Okay," I relented. "I guess I can have the night off."

"Wonderful. I'll be at your place in an hour. Pack an overnight bag."

Before I could question him he'd rung off. I dropped my mobile to the bed and sat in shocked silence for a moment.

"Shit, an hour?" I screamed and scrambled out of my bed. I had to get a move on if I wanted to be presentable when he arrived to pick me up. I had to ring Taylor too and I had to pack. What would I need? I contemplated wearing the corset Darren had bought me since it was easily my sexiest item of clothing but I decided against it in the end. I would feel weird wearing it and I knew Greg would go mad if he found out I was wearing a gift from his greatest rival.

I'd just stuffed the last item in my case when there was a buzz at the door.

"Who is it?" I asked, pressing the call button as I shrugged myself into a coat.

"It's Chester, miss, Mr Stamford's driver. Are you ready?"

"I'll be down in a moment, Chester, thank you."

"Okay, miss. The car is just out front. Oh, and Mr Stamford told me to make sure you'd packed your passport."

"My passport?"

"Yes, miss."

"Oh, all right. I'll get it now. I'll be out in a minute."

I'd just had a conversation with a man's driver. How weird was that? And why would I need my passport?

Luckily it was in the cupboard where I expected it to be and I was out of my flat within a few minutes. I was lightheaded with it all. I was excited to see Greg and really intrigued about his plans for us.

"Hello, miss." I was greeted politely by Chester. He took my bag and opened the car door. I didn't know what type it was, just black, sleek with a leather interior. I knew it wasn't a limousine or a Mini but that was about as definite as I could get. Cars didn't do anything for me and like many people in the capital I didn't own one—the Tube was a much quicker mode of transportation.

"Hey." I slid into the car and greeted Greg.

Greg didn't reply, he just leaned in and kissed me. Hard, raw and passionate, his lips on mine aroused a deep lust that whirled around my insides, making me dizzy and quickening my pulse. The driver's side door opening and shutting pulled me back to reality. I leaned back and my lips left Greg's with an audible pop.

"You missed me then." I laughed to cover my embarrassment at being caught in the middle of a tryst by the driver. Greg seemed unmoved.

"I might have, just a little." He smiled. "It seems you got under my skin."

I blushed with the sincerity of his words.

"So, where are you taking me?" I asked.

"Hotel Plaza Athenee."

"Erm, where?" The place sounded very posh. It wasn't a hotel I was familiar with and I knew a lot of the ones in London because we often recommended accommodation for our guests.

"Paris." He didn't flicker an eyelid.

"Paris, France?" My eyebrows shot up into my hairline.

"Yes, is there another?"

"I have to be back in work tomorrow," I blurted. "I can't leave Taylor more than one night on his own!"

"It's fine, we'll be back by lunch tomorrow."

Apparently Greg was used to popping across the Channel willy-nilly. I took a deep breath and attempted to relax. I had no reason to disbelieve him, I was sure we'd be back in time. I texted my second-in-command just in case—I wasn't going to let my business suffer because some billionaire was whisking me away to the city of lovers on a whim.

The airport went past in a blur. There was little waiting, next to no paperwork then suddenly I was on a tiny little plane in a huge, white leather chair sipping champagne and nibbling on gourmet treats with caviar and fine smoked salmon.

"So, you have your own plane, I should have guessed."

"Of course." He nodded. "In my business you need to get about."

"How long will it take to get to Paris?"

"Not long." He caressed the stem of his glass. I wanted him to caress me. Just being close to him made my skin tingle. Just looking at him had me wet and wanting. "I think it's maybe an hour or so."

I nodded and stretched out in my seat. "This is definitely a great way to travel."

"Mm, I know an even better way to pass the time, though."

"Oh yes? You got Monopoly on board?" I winked cheekily.

He laughed, the chuckle blooming from deep in his stomach, the sound rich and earthy when the mirth eventually exited his lips.

"I may have, but my idea is better than that." He leaned over the arm that separated us and I moved closer to him.

"Really? That good?"

"Oh, yeah." He kissed me, wrapped his arms around my shoulders and pulled me in close. My breasts squished against his warm chest and my stomach crushed up close against the seat arm.

"What about the steward?" I asked. The lovely gentleman had popped the champagne and served the snacks. I was worried he'd walk back through at any moment.

"He'll stay in the back until I call him and I'm not going to call him any time soon."

"Well, okay." I continued to kiss him with the sound of engines in the background and a slight unease in my stomach from being in close proximity to Greg as much as being in flight. I knew I was off the ground, I felt floatier somehow, but Greg's kiss grounded me. I wanted to get even closer but then he pulled back with a pop.

"Trust me," he said, and slipped down off his chair onto the floor. I did wonder for a brief moment if he'd gone completely off his rocker but then I felt his knees tapping at my shoe ends so I widened my thighs. His fingers wandered up the inside of my naked legs and under the hem of the short skirt I wore. A tad impractical for a cold autumn day, but I'd not noticed a lack of heat, and now the temperature was soaring.

When Greg's questing led him to the edge of my knickers he simply hooked the material to one side. He insinuated his whole body between my spread thighs, his head ducked under the fabric of my skirt. I could just see his movement under the material if I looked closely at my lap. I scooted my butt closer to the edge of the chair and spread my thighs wider. Greg plunged his tongue between my folds and eagerly lapped up the juices pooling there. The arousal was intense—his lapping was frenzied but expert as he hit my clit over and over, causing whimpers to escape from my throat unbidden. I came hard and fast, still surprised by his actions. He didn't give me time to recover, though. He crawled out from under the table and sat on the thick cream carpet. He beckoned me over with a finger.

I slipped down onto the carpet and crawled over. I wondered if he could see mischief shining in my eyes.

"On the floor?" I whispered, crawling nearer him. "Really?"

"Yes, the good thing about being a billionaire is you can do what you want wherever you want, and I want you here now." He kissed me briefly—I could taste my musk on his lips. Then he pushed me over onto my back and I yelped in shock. The sound mellowed into a giggle of surprise. He wasted no time. He pulled a condom from a packet on the side of the chair nearest to us.

"Always prepared," Greg said. I pulled down his trousers while he fiddled with the condom. His cock was hard and throbbing, deep pink nearing red at the tip. It left me breathless and wanting more even after my explosively good orgasm of moments earlier. He sheathed himself confidently then without a moment's hesitation he took me.

Greg slammed into me. His dick stretched my eager walls around him. He didn't take it slowly, he banged into me with force and determination. I curled myself around him, grabbed his shoulders and gripped his hips with my thighs. I clung on as he hit my sensitized clit with his pubis over and over, every touch sending paroxysms of pleasure through every inch of me. It wasn't long, it wasn't pretty but it was one of the most memorable fucks of my life. When he came it was with a roar and when he softened he slipped from within me and lay next to me, spent on the floor. We panted in harmony.

"Better get up," Greg said a few moments later. "We'll be coming into land soon."

* * * *

The hotel was astounding, the suite we were in was opulent but comfortable and the little balcony had a view out toward the Eiffel Tower. It was perfectly romantic.

"What a view," I sighed. I leaned against the edge of the steel scrollwork of the balustrade and felt the autumn breeze ruffle my hair. I was a little cold, but I didn't mind. I was in awe of the vista, the sprawling city with quaint corner cafés and pretty white houses, tall and thin and elegant. I'd always dreamed of visiting Paris—I only wished I could stay longer.

When I looked over my shoulder to find where Greg was because he hadn't answered, I saw him pacing up and down past the golden scrolled fireplace with his mobile pressed to his ear. It was clearly a business call. I felt momentarily disgruntled, but then I shrugged it off. He was a billionaire businessman, would he really stop his work just because of me?

A wicked idea crossed my mind and before I really thought I turned around. I walked back into the room and slipped off my shoes. He hadn't noticed me, so I cleared my throat. He looked up to see me unfastening the top buttons of my blouse. His eyebrows raised but he continued to talk into the phone.

"Can't Robertson deal with it?"

I sashayed closer to him, hips swaying as buttons unfastened surprisingly easily between my shaking fingers. At six feet away from him I dropped the blouse from my shoulders and fiddled with the fastening on my skirt.

Greg's gaze was fixed firmly on me. His voice rose.

"Look, Victor, I have left you in charge, so you need to deal with it. Yes, I know what I told you but now I'm telling you to deal with it your bloody self!"

Greg licked his lips. I dropped the skirt from my hips and I took another step toward him. I was bold, I was brave. Maybe it was something in the air because when I reached him, I entwined my arms around his shoulders and whispered into the ear unoccupied by a phone, "I want you to fuck me now. I'll be waiting in the bedroom."

I stalked away from him, heart thumping, and as I moved I slipped the material of my knickers down over my buttocks and let them fall from me before stepping out of them and into the bedroom.

"Look, I've got something more urgent to deal with. Just go with your gut, I'll call you later."

I scurried into the bedroom, pulled off my bra in a hurry and threw myself onto the bed which bounced back joyfully and enveloped me in warm, luxurious comfort.

"Wicked, naughty girl." I looked up to see Greg striding across to the bed, his shirt part removed and his hand on his belt buckle. "I should spank you for distracting me like that."

"What?" I asked, coquettishly fluttering my lashes. "I did nothing."

The clunk of his trousers to the floor and the addition of his weight to the bed made my stomach leap with anticipation.

"Nothing, wench? You could well have just caused the downfall of my company."

"Oh, no," I squealed as he grabbed my naked waist and pulled me to him. "I merely gave you a suggestion."

"A suggestion I'd have been mad to refuse," he growled then kissed me hard, crushing the breath from my lungs.

"Well," I gasped when he let me up for air, "I have always been good at providing a convincing argument."

"Indeed"—he nodded, a sparkle of mischief in his eye—"and I am good at providing suitable punishment for bratty, beautiful girls like you."

He pulled me toward him. I yelped and sprawled across his lap, his erection digging into my stomach, my hands dangling down the side of the bed, my legs wrapped in the mussed up blankets.

"Oh no," I gasped. "Don't spank me!"

I'd never been spanked, never seen the attraction. As I waited there under the control of a hard, ruthless and gloriously handsome man I started to realize what I might have been missing.

"Nope, you deserve it. Stop wiggling," he commanded and slapped my buttocks. The impact stung but excited. I yelped. Greg stroked my arse and whispered gently, "If it's too much, darling, shout 'Diamonds' and I'll stop immediately."

I nodded, touched by his caring words, then thrilled by the crack of his hard hand on my soft, giving flesh once more.

"Tell me you're sorry," he growled, hitting me once more. It hurt. He wasn't holding back. I was tempted to shout out in my shock but I didn't because beneath the pain and the embarrassment was the prickle of pleasure and the anticipation of more.

"No," I gasped, the heat of my arse rolling through my body, making me glow with ecstasy.

"I will not stop"—he punctuated each word with a spank—"until you say sorry, you naughty, naughty, wicked, temptingly wonderful woman."

"I'm sorry," I gasped, grinding my hips against him, the hot, harsh bloom of pain diffusing into the hot throb of desire. "I'm so sorry."

"And so you should be." He stopped spanking. My arse ached more with need than the pain of impact. I wanted him to continue. "Now get up here and kiss me, so we can make up and fuck."

"Yes, sir." I brought myself up on hands and knees then lifted back until my buttocks skimmed my heels. The pressure against my reddened skin made me squint and tighten up but then he leaned in and kissed me and I melted into Greg's embrace. He wiggled down onto the bed and pulled me over him.

"Condom," I squeaked, my words almost refusing to leave my lips. I was eager to fuck but not that eager.

"Got it." Greg slipped his hand beneath the top pillow and pulled out a small, square packet. I assumed he'd put it there earlier—either that or this place had run out of chocolate mints. I kissed him and he reached beneath my body to cover himself. He barely struggled, confidently sheathing himself and doing battle with me, lip to lip and tongue to tongue.

I settled down onto him, his cock embedding within me, stretching and arousing me, combining with the ache in my arse to consume me with bliss. I moved instinctively, my mind addled with ecstasy. I lifted and fell, my hands resting on the pillow beside his head, his hands gripped tightly on my hips. My eyes closed, unable to fight the weight of pleasure pulling them down.

Sparks of orgasmic enjoyment erupted at every impact of crotch against crotch, and gasps, pants and moans from both of us merged together in harmony. I felt Greg laboring beneath me, lifting his hips to push him deeper into me to get more purchase. I flicked open my eyes and watched him. His cheeks were red and rosy, his lips parted and his eyes were screwed up tightly. He looked vulnerable, sexy and real and I felt a pang of something deeper than lust that intensified when his eyelids fluttered open. He met my gaze and smiled—his face was transformed with it. I read something there, something fleeting, something deep that sent a jolt of enjoyable fear through me. I closed my eyes, unable to take the intensity, and he screamed roughly, held himself deep within me as he came.

I melted in a puddle beside him, still fizzing with sexual tension but happy not to climax. I had come once that day anyway and I was pleased to have pulled him from his business to provide him with some pleasure. So I was surprised when he turned toward me, kissed my cheek and ran his hand down my front. He swept over my breasts, fingers tickling my nipples and eliciting a soft moan from between my lips. His touch drifted lower, skimmed the curve of my stomach and dipped between my thighs. I spread them a little wider. Greg's thick fingers tickled over my pubic hair hinting that maybe I was still open for more. I was. Where moments earlier I'd been sated and satisfied with what gratification I'd gotten, with the sweep of his touch along my body I was once again alive with desire.

I wondered if he was merely teasing because his fingers stopped just short of my clit. I wanted to whimper and moan, to plead for release, but my pride wouldn't let me. I opened my eyes and looked up, crooking my neck slightly so I met his gaze. He had his head propped on one hand, offering him a good view along the length of my body.

I tingled under his appreciative stare. I didn't pull away from it. I held my breath as I waited for his reply to my voiceless challenge. Inside my mind I was goading him to make me come, laying down the orgasmic gauntlet. I wished the words would force out of my mouth but the power in his dark eyes locked them away deep inside me. I wasn't the one in control, I just had to wait to see what his next whim would be. I was pliant and frustrated all at the same time and couldn't have been more thankful when his fingertips grazed my clit.

I closed my eyes and pleasure tore through me, centering my attention on the fingers that explored me. Greg took his time stroking my slippery folds. Weak and painfully turned on, I didn't have the energy to lift a limb, to move my body, to direct him to what I wanted. I lay compliant beneath him as his lips tickled my collarbone in time with his seeking digits.

By the time his kisses rolled down to my nipples I was hanging on the very edge of ecstasy. I knew that just a few well-positioned strokes would bring me to climax. I wanted it desperately, but at the same time I didn't want it. I didn't want the tension, the anticipation to end. I was so sexually alive and I felt so good being out of control for once. I wanted it to go on forever, even if I would expire from the pressure building up inside me to come.

Greg sucked my nipple hard and slid his fingers to my clit. I tightened, anticipating the last moment of want, eagerly awaiting the breaking climax. He surprised me once more by resting his finger there on top of my wet need and lifting away from my nipple. My eyes flicked open and his face was above mine. His focus drifted from my eyes to my lips and back again. He was taking in every aspect of my visage.

"Come for me." He said those three words, gently, deeply but with such command that as he pressed my clit and rubbed once and just before he completed the next sweep the ecstasy swamped me. I felt the swathe of his fingertip and I shuddered and twisted beneath him. His upper body pressed down on me as his lips met mine. He sucked on the orgasmic gratification that poured from my body and it transferred from my body to his, like a wave. He then passed it back with the movements of his lips and the stilling of his fingers. The intensity of pleasure lessened as we batted it between us, lip to lip, finger to clit.

I gasped deeply when he pulled out of the kiss, desperate for oxygen and stability. We lay still, atmosphere heavy, bodies replete. I could feel the need to say things, to whisper sweet nothings—this was the point to do that. But when I rolled over, ready to say something potentially stupid, he rolled the other way and perched on the edge of the bed.

"I better check that my company still exists, but I'll be back for you soon, my wicked temptress."

I smiled then and swallowed the words that had bubbled up inside.

* * * *

I soon persuaded myself it had been silliness, a response to the ecstasy that had streamed through my body. The short trip passed in a whirl of shopping, eating and fucking. It was glorious but when we were out I felt the gaze of the world on my shoulders. I felt a little like I was being paraded around like a prized pet. I didn't know if Greg thought of me like that—he never professed anything deeper than lust for me, even there in the city of lovers.

I felt a sadness creep over me when I got home. I got back into the swing of work and loved that, as always, but when I got home each night—well, early hours of the morning—I felt the loneliness of an empty apartment more keenly. Remembering the encounters with Greg and of course Darren didn't remove any of that.

Chapter Five

"So, sweet cheeks, what have you got planned for today?"

I shook my head against my mobile and sighed. "Work, Darren, it's Saturday night."

"You're the boss, can't you—?"

"No, I can't," I snapped before he finished his sentence. I hadn't slept well since returning from Paris earlier in the week. Something weighed heavy on my heart but I was reluctant to inspect it further to find out what it was.

"All right, fair enough, love," he sighed. "Maybe another time, then?"

"Yeah, maybe." My tone and my resolve softened when I heard the disappointment in his voice. He was only trying to be nice to me after all.

I forgot the conversation soon enough in the hubbub of that night. We had a birthday party to cater on top of the usual rush for food and drinks and a good old time. I was a barman down to flu and a nasty virus had wiped out several of my waiting staff. I divided my time between the two, filling in the gaps. I might have been the boss but I was just a member of staff like any other and I mucked in when needed to make things work. I was knackered by eleven and although food service had ended and it was relatively quiet I knew it wouldn't last. Saturday night saw the clubbers turn out in force. We would be packed to the rafters again within the hour.

"Jen, could you stay on and tend bar?" I asked one of the waitresses as she walked past.

"Oh, boss, you know I would usually but—" She patted her tummy, which was a little more protruding than usual. I then remembered why I hadn't asked her to do any overtime for a while.

"Oh, I'm sorry, I forgot in the madness of it all. How are you feeling?"

"Not bad," she replied. "Morning sickness is over at last, thank God. It's the swollen ankles that do my head in now, but still, won't be long till the little sprout makes an appearance."

"No, not long. We need to meet about your maternity leave… Before you go could you just ask the others if any of them want to do the bar tonight? I'll give them time and a half for it."

"Sure, boss, I'll ask."

I knew I was lucky. I had a good body of staff—yes, I had a relatively high turnover, since many of them were students and eventually they'd go off to seek long-term employment, but I could rely on my team to go the extra mile. People were happy to work in Diamonds. I suspected the high tips from wealthy patrons had more to do with it than the firm but fair boss, but it all worked and that was the main thing.

"Well, hello," a familiar voice roused me from my thoughts. "I didn't have you down as a barmaid."

"Hi, Darren." I smiled stiffly. "We're short-staffed tonight."

"Bummer," he sighed. "I was hoping to whisk you away for a night of hot loving."

"No chance, darling. Sorry." I shrugged, and passed the pint I'd pulled to the skinny man stood beside Darren. I took the money and passed back the change. I wished Darren wasn't there. As much as I liked the guy, I didn't have time for small talk.

"Do you need a barman?" he asked.

"Tonight, yes, we're a server down." I took the next order, two pretty drinks for the small, pretty lady in red.

"Good job I'm here, then. Move over."

"What?" I looked up to see him slipping over to my side of the bar.

"I was a barman for years when I was at uni. I'll give you a hand." He smiled, leaned over the bar and took the next person's order.

"I hope you know what you're doing," I sighed, opening the till.

"Sure I do. Where's your price list?"

I pointed down to the cheat sheet we kept below the bar for trainees. Darren nodded.

I shook my head and carried on serving. If he didn't get under my feet or seriously upset a customer I supposed there was no harm in letting him help out for the evening.

He turned out to be very capable, an absolute godsend in fact. The customers thought it was brilliant, being served by a billionaire. Darren posed for many photos and kept the people who were waiting for drinks entertained. We had zero complaints from the moment he hopped to my side of the bar.

"So, Mr Bennett, are you looking for a full-time job?" I looked up from the glasses I was putting away as he walked by.

"Why, are you offering me one?"

"On tonight's performance I certainly think I should. You were great."

"Aw, shucks. I'm flattered but, and don't take this the wrong way, I don't think you can afford my wages."

"You're telling me ten quid an hour doesn't draw you in?"

"Naw, I make closer to ten thousand quid an hour, so I'll pass. But I did enjoy myself tonight."

"Good. You really helped me out tonight. Thank you."

"You're welcome, sweetie. Now, about that payment, can I take it in kind?"

He brushed up close and I put the tumbler down just before it fell from my shaking fingertips. "Well, I have a couple of kilos of assorted bar snacks in the store..." I winked.

"That's not quite what I meant." Darren grabbed me and pressed his lips to mine before I had time to protest or to check if anyone was watching. I was incensed and turned on all at the same time so I didn't push him away for a few seconds.

"Darren," I snapped, "stop messing about. Someone could see."

"Are you ashamed of me?" He looked hurt and that surprised me.

"No, but I'm the boss here, I don't want my employees gossiping about me behind my back."

He shrugged then kissed me again.

"No one's here," he answered as I banged on his chest. "I sent them all home with a generous tip and a smile."

"You sent my staff home?"

"Yep." He nodded and ran a finger down my cleavage. I took a step back and the bar struck the middle of my back.

"Without asking me?"

"Indeed." He stepped forward and placed his hands on my hips.

"And you expect me to be okay with that?" I was angry. I was the one in control when I was at work. I was the boss, I made the decisions, no one else. I was pissed off but I couldn't stop myself appreciating his musk-like scent and the bulge in his trousers that he pushed against my hip.

"Not really," he continued, "but I was hoping that a good shag would make you forget all about it, or at least make you not care about it." Darren smirked irritatingly and squeezed his hands up over my waist to cup my breasts through the cotton of my work T-shirt.

"Do you think I'm that shallow?" I was losing the plot of why I was mad with him, but I was clinging to the fact that he'd upset me and there must have been a good reason behind it, even if everything within me was crying out for me just to stop thinking and fuck him.

"No, but I'm ever hopeful."

"Seems that hope's about to pay off," I whispered then kissed him. I didn't have any excuse or any resistance. I shouldn't have done it, I was sure there was a very good reason to not kiss the hot man in front of me but I couldn't see it for the hot man in front of me. He tasted delicious. Sweet, salty and addictive. Once I'd started kissing I didn't want to stop.

He pressed harder against me, ran his hands up under my top and confidently stroked over my cotton-covered breasts. Darren clearly had no doubt he'd get his way. I could sense it in every stroke and in the curve of his smile as we kissed. He was a man used to getting his way and I was no match for his arousal. Strangely, that turned me on all the more. I was happy to be at his mercy. He didn't use ropes or bindings to tie me down, though. Just the weight of his body against me as he eased his hand down into my work trousers and day-to-day cotton knickers beneath.

"You're soaked," his words escaped breathily and tickled my ear. He gently caressed my clitoris. "You've wanted this all along, wicked girl."

I moaned and slumped into him, my legs wobbling beneath me as I forgot to hold up my weight in the onslaught of sexual arousal. I wanted to fight back, insist that I didn't want him to be taking control in my bar, but I couldn't get the words out past the tumult of desire that raged through every cell and completely absorbed all the energy of my brain.

"I'm going to fuck you now," he announced and I heard the crinkle of a packet being withdrawn from his trouser pocket. "Turn around."

He stepped back and I steadied myself with a hand on the bar. After a deep breath I opened my eyes. Darren had unbuckled his belt and his expensive chinos flowed down his legs to pool around his ankles. I could see his erection straining against the cotton of his briefs and I licked my lips in anticipation.

"Come on, turn around," he growled, "and lose the pants."

I loved the rough command, though something deep within me prickled at being ordered about in the sanctity of my own place. I bit it down and turned around. I fiddled with the button on my trousers and with trembling fingers freed myself from them and the damp knickers beneath.

"Lean across the bar," he said at the same time that he grabbed my hip and made me jump. He'd startled me. I hadn't realized he was so close. I followed his instructions. He played with my arse. He cupped my buttocks in his warm hands then squeezed like he was testing the springiness of a cushion. He traced patterns with his fingertips, dipping into the cleft between my cheeks and tickling at my vulva, teasing and taunting me as I clung onto the wooden edge of the cold bar for dear life. I wanted him to spank me. I remembered back to Paris and Greg's hard hand imprinting on my soft bottom and I wanted more of that. I tried not to get tied up with guilt at remembering another man while fucking Darren. It was only sex and why shouldn't I fuck two hot billionaires if I wanted to?

Luckily Darren pushed those thoughts from my mind when he held me open and drove his cock into me. I was disappointed to not feel the sting of his hand on my bum but that was soon overpowered by the satisfaction of having him inside me. My molten heat soon warmed the cooler sheath of the condom covering him and when he moved my juices clung and I could hear the sucking of my eager pussy in the stillness of the empty club.

A lewd, base noise that turned me on, it was soon joined by Darren's grunts and my own as well as the slap of flesh on flesh when he hammered into me. No finesse, no softness or romance, he just fucked me and I held on tightly as he pounded me. Sparks of semi-orgasms blazed through me. The friction of him at that angle seemed to hit all my internal hotspots and I was gliding on euphoria even though he held my hips in his bruising tight grip to keep his dick deep within me. I felt the spasm and pump of his flesh resting against my sensitized walls and my cunt clutched in time with his release.

He gently stroked my back then pulled away from me. By the time I'd turned around he'd pulled up his trousers and was just pulling his belt tight around his waist. I wasn't satisfied—yes, I had felt tremors of ecstasy but I needed more. Darren was oblivious to that.

"Fantastic fuck," he said, dropping the filled condom into the bin beside him. "We'll have to do it again sometime."

He blew me a kiss and walked away.

"Erm, yeah," I stuttered through my confusion. "See you, Darren."

I followed him to the door once I'd realized what was happening and I'd pulled myself into my own trousers. I locked the door behind him and finished off the clean-down alone. Darren had dismissed all my staff to shag me but hadn't bothered to stay to help me clean up the mess that was left after their dismissal. What a selfish fucking bastard.

I thoroughly beat myself up mentally as I mopped, wiped and emptied bins. I ran on empty and stumbled back home. I didn't remember getting on the Tube. I didn't remember getting into bed. I slept.

* * * *

The buzzing of the door alarm aroused me. I groaned, rolled over and tried to ignore it but someone had their finger jammed on the button and wasn't letting go. I looked over at my clock through half-open eyes, blinked and groaned again. It was only eight o'clock—that was the middle of the night for a club worker like me.

I stumbled out of bed and stomped to the intercom.

"Yes, what do you want?" I snapped.

"You," the familiar, deep mellow voice replied. "Good morning, Kerry."

"Morning, Greg," I responded sweetly. "Piss off, would you?"

"Aw, come on." I could hear the pout even if I couldn't see it. "I came all this way for you, Kerry, please let me in."

"Urgh." I rubbed the sleep from my eyes and ran my hand into my hair. "I'm tired, Greg. I didn't get in from the club till God knows what hour. I'm grumpy, I'm probably stinky and I'm certainly not sexy. Are you sure you want to come in?"

I just hoped no one else could hear the conversation because it would be blasting out of the intercom into the busy street. Although how busy it would be I didn't know, I never left my flat until mid-afternoon.

"Yes, I really want to come in. Please? I promise I'll be good."

"Yeah," I laughed, pressing the button to let him in. "I'll believe that when I see it."

I opened the door then immediately trailed back into my bedroom. A stupid thing to do, all in all, but my brain ached and I just wanted to get back to sleep. A few moments later I heard the door close and the clump of heavy footsteps across my living room.

I waited for the bedroom door to open, but it didn't. I crinkled my brow in confusion, then shrugged, snuggled down under my duvet and surprisingly quickly fell back to sleep.

* * * *

Next time I woke up it was past midday and I felt much more like myself. I got up, stretched, ran my fingers through my unruly hair and slipped my feet into my slippers. My stomach rumbled as I caught the scent of bacon on the air. I figured the guy next door was having his usual Sunday fried brunch — I'd often been able to smell his culinary delights from my room. I'd been tempted a time or two to knock on his door and see if he needed help eating the delicious-smelling food, but I'd resisted and stuck to my toast and cereal and exciting ready meals for one. I could cook, I just never had the time to do so — or to enjoy a leisurely meal with my neighbor, come to that.

I was intensely surprised when I walked into my living room and it was suspiciously clean. Mrs Morris usually came in on a Monday and tidied for me — I'd decided early on in my club-running days that I didn't have enough hours in the day to clean a house and a business, so I employed the mum of one of my bar staff to keep the flat under control. It was Sunday, my place shouldn't have been so tidy. I was fairly certain that I'd left a pile of magazines on the end of my sofa and that there'd been the remnants of breakfast on the coffee table too. I'd certainly not left the throws so straight and the bin so empty. The puzzle was soon solved, though.

"Morning, sunshine. Well, afternoon, actually. Would you like some pancakes?" Greg smiled at me from the kitchenette at the other end of the room. He had on my rarely used floral pinny — a present from an aunty at Christmas—and was standing at my cooker, a frying pan in hand.

"Erm, well, yes," I stuttered. "Yes please, Greg." It took a moment for my mind to register what had happened while I was still mostly asleep. I'd let Greg in earlier and he'd apparently kept himself busy.

"Okey-dokey, it'll be ready in a minute."

He turned back to the stove and flipped, elegantly, a thin crêpe. I shook my head. I was certain I was still dreaming. Sitting heavily in the chair closest to me, I started to babble.

"I'm sorry I was so ratty to you before. I was just tired. It'd been a long night then I left you all on your own. You should have gone home. You certainly didn't have to do all this." I waved my hand around expansively like I was swatting at flies. "My cleaner comes in tomorrow."

"It's fine"—he smiled—"I enjoy this kind of thing and I don't often get time for it. You were clearly tired. I did look into your room when I arrived but you were completely tuckered out. So I kept myself entertained."

He walked toward me with a tray in hand. On one plate were two neatly rolled pancakes, decorated with slices of strawberries and icing sugar. On the other lay scrambled eggs, bacon and half a grilled tomato. There was another rarely used present from my aunt in the center, a metal toast rack filled with slices of toast, a small ramekin of butter sitting in front of it.

"Well, you have been busy," I gasped. "Thank you."

"I didn't know what you'd want." His tanned cheeks flushed crimson. "So I made a few things."

He rushed back to the kitchen and came back with his own plate of food and two glasses of orange juice.

"You've been shopping too," I chuckled. "I didn't have any of this food in."

"Well, sort of." He sat on the sofa opposite me and took a bite of his toast, chewed, smiled and continued. "I got Chester to bring it all over for me."

I shook my head and continued to eat.

"This is quite the surrealest breakfast experience of my life so far," I giggled, still unsure of how it had all come together. I honestly felt like I was dreaming.

"It's pretty unusual for me too," Greg confessed, sitting back and sipping from his glass, "but also the most pleasant breakfast I've had in a long time."

It was my turn to blush, so I picked up a piece of toast and buttered it. Leaning my head forward meant my cheeks were covered with my hair.

"Aren't you busy with work? Last time we spoke you said you didn't anticipate getting a break until next week."

"Well, yeah. I am really busy but currently I'm waiting to hear back from another company and until I get word there's not much else I can do on this deal." Greg looked the most relaxed I'd ever seen him, sitting there on my sofa and eating the breakfast he'd just prepared for us. He had on dark denim jeans and a bright white T-shirt, which didn't have a spot of food on it. If I cooked, I ended up with more of the ingredients on me than in the pan.

We chatted and ate, indulging in a deeply intimate and domestic scene. Unbidden, the memory of what Darren and I had gotten up to in the bar the night before crept up on me and guilt lay in the pit of my stomach. How did women do it? Juggle more than one man? If I could just keep my emotions separate like I kept the boys apart then it would all be okay, but as I looked at Greg and tried to take in all he told me, all I could feel was the imprint of Darren's hands on my hips.

"Oh, I'm full." I made a show of patting my tummy when Greg had finished his tale. I put down my cutlery and sat back on the chair. "Thanks so much for that."

"You're welcome." He got to his feet.

"Oh no, please, I'll tidy up. It's the least I can do."

"No, I made the mess, I'll clean it." He grinned. "You just disappear into that bedroom and prepare yourself for a damn good fucking because, Kerry, I am desperate for you."

How do you answer a statement like that? I was stunned and horny, very horny.

"Oh, I'll go for a quick shower then." I finally strung together something approaching a sentence. "Hurry up, though. I'm desperate for you too."

I rushed into my room and the en suite, dropped my clothes then slipped into the shower and switched on the water. I danced from foot to foot as I waited for it to warm up. I felt the icy blasts and wished they'd erase the guilt I felt over fucking Darren the night before.

As the water warmed I berated myself. I was being silly—I wasn't in a relationship with Greg or Darren. I was a free agent and it was fine for me to enjoy myself with both of the billionaires. Like buses, you wait for a hot, rich man to sweep you off your feet and two come along at once. I laughed bitterly and scrubbed at my skin.

I had forced thoughts of Darren to the back of my mind until I saw the bruise over my left hip. I didn't know exactly what had caused it but I was certain it'd happened the night before.

I stared at it for a while, scrubbed at it, even though it hurt, and wished it'd disappear. Why couldn't I forget Darren? I had Greg right there with me. I told myself to stop being silly and focus on one tasty man at a time.

I turned off the shower and dried myself. I had just slipped into a light silken nightie when Greg walked in. I was glad I'd spent a few minutes sweeping up all my strewn, dirty clothes into the laundry basket since he'd already tidied up the rest of the flat for me. I was worried he'd want to clean my bedroom too and maybe he'd change his mind about fucking me.

"Hey." He walked across the room toward me.

"Hey," I replied and felt the heat sweep up my neck and across my cheeks. He appraised me and the short, slinky shift I was wearing. I felt vulnerable and weak as he visually devoured me inch by inch.

"God, you're gorgeous," he growled. He pulled me into him and held me tight.

I let out a deep, shuddering breath of relief when my insecurities stopped screaming in the back of my mind and I let myself enjoy the feel of his arms around me.

"I'm so glad you think so," I whispered and kissed the skin just above his collarbone, "because you're so hot I just want to grab you and hold you and do wicked things to you every single time I see you."

"Really?" He moved a strong arm from around me and used a finger to tip up my chin and bring my gaze to meet his.

"Yes, really," I replied. My heart thumped erratically. I didn't know why I'd felt the need to confess such a thing, and I worried that maybe it was too much, that maybe I sounded a bit crazy stalkerish.

"Brilliant, it seems we're completely in sync, because every time I see you I want you to do nasty things to me and with me. On top of me and under me. I'm glad we're on the same page."

He kissed me. His hand slid down my throat and rested on my breast as our lips ravaged each other, our tongues pressed forward and each sought dominance. Lust took over and thought and words became unnecessary. The brief covering I'd just put on he pulled off in a second and he pushed me down onto the bed before I could protest or even attempt to pull his top off. He pushed me over onto the center of the bed and joined me there.

He was fully clothed and I felt the scratch of his clothes like a frustrating barrier between us. He kissed along my neck and collarbone and I brought my hands round to try to wrestle him out of his top.

"Stop it," he commanded. "You're distracting me."

"But I want you naked," I blurted. "I'm naked, it's not fair."

"I like it this way," he said. "Now hush and let me kiss you all over."

I let my hands fall back above my head and he continued kissing a trail along my body. I writhed beneath him, his lips soft and hot dragging lust up from my core to suffuse every last cell in my body. I wasn't thinking, so when he captured my aching left nipple between his teeth, I brought my arms down from over my head and bunched my fingers up in the pristine white of his T-shirt.

"What did I tell you?" he growled and most disappointingly stopped kissing me.

"Erm..." I strived to remember but my mind was blank. All I could think about was how much I wanted him.

"You really are a naughty, naughty thing." He shook his head then winked. His smile could only have been described as sardonic as he reached down to the floor and picked up my lingerie.

"Put your hands up."

"Is this a stick-up?" I giggled, unable to resist the pun.

"Yes, can't you feel my concealed weapon?" He pushed his crotch down on mine and I could feel how hard he was in there. I gulped.

"Okay, mister, I'll come quietly, don't hurt me." I lifted my hands above my head and played along.

"Very good, but I'm pretty certain you'll come loudly, young lady." He grinned and tied my wrists together with the wisp of silk that had covered me moments earlier. I lay there, completely open to him, unable to cover myself from his sight, unable to touch him, to stop him. I was completely at his mercy.

I had never been so wet and ready in my whole life before.

"Same rules as last time," he whispered as he moved in to kiss my earlobe. "Just yell 'Diamonds' if I do anything you want to stop."

I nodded and he continued to kiss down my neck. His clothes-covered body scraped sensuously over my sensitized skin when he got back to the business of kissing me all over. And he meant *all* over. Under my arms, my elbows and my fingers all felt the caress of his lips. My neck, throat and collarbone, the flat of my chest and the hillocks of my breasts were all covered with kisses and nibbles as his hard, heavy body pressed against me and teased me without giving any satisfaction whatsoever.

I was a slave to his whim and I swore I would come if he just breathed on my clit, I was so wound up. It was wonderful. No one had ever taken such time to tease and arouse me. He nibbled my nipples and sucked each one until I sobbed and crooned his name.

And still he meticulously kissed lower. He didn't rush over my stomach, he tickled my belly button and ran his hands over the soft swell. His lips followed and as he sank lower a gentle moan escaped his lips and caressed my flesh.

I was sure he could smell my arousal. He worshiped every little freckle and traced the faint stretch marks that I hate with his fingers. He showed no repulsion when he kissed them and I felt a blossom of something warm and tender in my chest when he stroked and soothed me. It was like he was trying to remember every inch of my body, so he could call it to mind at any moment, and that excited me.

"Oh, baby, where'd you get this bruise?" He gently stroked it then kissed gently over that betraying mark. I felt my cheeks flare with heat and I was glad he wasn't looking at my face as I knew guilt was written all over it.

"I don't know." I shrugged as far as I could with my arms stretched above my head. I could have moved them down, it just hadn't crossed my mind to do so. "I guess I must have bumped it at work last night. It was completely manic."

"I'll kiss it all better." His voice reverberated over my skin as he kept his promise. He continued lower, skipped over the one place I wanted him to stay and linger, and took his time licking and kissing every inch of each leg. I tried so hard to guide his mouth to my clit. I bumped my hips up and down, strained high to get him to give me some relief, but he didn't. Not until he was ready.

I wasn't sure how he managed to lie so flat along the bed with the hard-on I knew was crushed inside his trousers. How he controlled himself so long at all I didn't understand. I was on the brink of losing it and still, apart from the ragged breathing and the soft moans of delight, he seemed to be unmoved.

He sank down between my thighs and I wantonly held myself open for him. I showed him my desire and hoped beyond hope that he'd satisfy my craving.

"You're so beautiful," he muttered, stroking my wet lips without touching my clit. "So pink and ripe and juicy. I just want to eat you all up."

"Please do," I begged. "Please, oh please…"

When his tongue swept along my pussy I thought I was going to explode with happiness. He held my thighs wide with his hands and licked and swirled his tongue over me until I writhed and screamed out his name.

"Greg, oh fuck, Greg," I moaned. My hands were still held above my head in surrender as surely as if they'd been tied there. Greg wanted them there so there they stayed. I was laid out for him, a sacrifice to his pleasure.

"Come for me." He broke contact with me and gasped, "Come for me, Kerry." Then he concentrated his mouth on my clit. He sucked and licked in rhythm until I couldn't help but give him what he wanted. A great flooding rush of an orgasm ripped me apart. Tears wetted my cheeks as the pleasure tore through me. I was completely awash with lust and something deeper than that, something that if I acknowledged it would scare me half to death.

"Fuck, I want you." He cursed and scrambled up between my thighs. I opened my eyes to see him staring down at me. I smiled weakly, too languorous to do anything with any real vigor. He returned the smile but there was something in his gaze that unsettled me—it was the first time I'd seen him truly undone in all the time we'd spent together.

He leaned forward and cupped my face in his hand and stroked away the tear that had dampened my cheek. His smile lengthened. I turned my head and kissed his thumb tip then. As I enveloped it with my mouth he closed his eyes and moaned with deep desire.

Pulling his thumb from between my lips with a pop, he set to undoing his pants and pushing them down his legs. He took a foil packet from the pocket and sheathed his hard, long erection before covering me completely with his body and pressing into me.

He was slow and gentle at first. My walls contracted around him as he slid deeper into my wet heat and when he moved I wrapped my legs around him and encouraged him deeper and deeper still with each thrust. From coiled control he turned into hammering desire, falling completely into the thrall of his lust as he sated himself on my body. Finally my bound hands fell down from their position above my neck to link around the back of his neck. I felt completely connected to him as he climbed closer to the brink of climax.

I watched when he came. His face screwed up in concentration and desire then released with the ecstasy that flowed from his body. I craned my neck and kissed him softly in thanks. He smiled in response then relaxed against me, burying his head in my shoulder. I remembered how little he'd smiled when we first met, how I'd been certain he didn't do it often. Yet he seemed to grin at me all the time when he was with me, now we'd been together a while.

We held there in that position for a long time. I was sexually sated but my spirit was agitated. Something special had just happened. It wasn't just about lust and passion, something deeper had blossomed between Greg and me. I didn't know if it was just me, though. Maybe Greg hadn't noticed it.

I wanted to say something, to explain what I felt, but I was too scared to do so. What if he'd not felt it at all? What if it was all in my imagination?

"Damn it, woman," Greg growled. "You completely blow my mind."

He extricated himself from my limbs and unfastened my wrists. He fastened his pants back up and I looked over at my clock.

"Shit, Greg, I've had an unbelievably good time but I should have been at Diamonds an hour ago!"

"And I should have rung Japan by now. You distracting minx. Let me ring Chester, he'll bring the car round and we'll give you a lift to work."

I didn't have any more time to contemplate the weirdness between us. Both of us were absorbed in dressing and getting out and getting to our places of work. Greg kissed me briefly as I left his car at the club.

"Thanks," he said and I looked at him in puzzlement.

"I should be thanking you, you did so much for me today."

"And you did so much for me, darling, See you soon."

I wondered for a moment if maybe he had felt it too, but then I entered the whirlwind of chaos that was my club without me at the helm and I put Greg to the back of my mind as far as I could.

Chapter Six

"So, I have a night off with a bad stomach and you replace me." Taylor didn't even say hello as I walked past him.

"What?" I snapped then remembered the temporary barman who had stepped in the night before. "Oh, no, it was just Darren mucking about, really. Saved my arse, though."

"Says here he's making it permanent." Taylor still sounded upset.

"Says where?"

"Here." He passed a tabloid newspaper to me.

"Fuck," I cursed. Right there in black and white was the craziest headline I'd ever seen. *Billionaire barman and his future wife?* And underneath a picture of me posing with Darren behind one of the beer pumps.

"So, which is it?" Taylor asked.

"Neither. Jeez, he just offered to help out, we were short-staffed... It seemed like a good idea at the time."

"My job's safe then?" Taylor asked in an easier tone.

"Sure it is, and everyone else's. This is just typical bloody tabloid shit. Ignore it."

"Right, boss, will do. Can I have my paper back now?"

"Yeah, of course. Now let's get down to work."

"You're a slave driver. Maybe I should contact Mr Bennett and see if he'd be less of a tyrant."

I slapped him and he giggled in a most unmanly manner.

"Joking, joking. You may be a tyrant but you're Diamonds' tyrant. I wouldn't have it any other way."

"Erm, thanks, I think."

I put the paper report to the back of my mind. I had to tell a few insistent journos to fuck off throughout the day—okay, so I was more polite than that, just. I had phone calls and questions fired at me in person. I didn't answer any of them. I knew whatever I said would be twisted to sound like whatever they wanted it to sound like anyway.

I was pissed off, but I supposed it wasn't Darren's fault really. He'd just been being nice. I should have realized something like this would have happened, but I'd never really thought of Darren as a celebrity. Obviously the rest of the world did. But it got our name out there and Diamonds certainly was busy for a Sunday, so maybe being on the front page was a good thing. Maybe I should thank Darren for it.

I dismissed that idea sharpish. I was still pissed off at him for using me the night before and being with Greg that morning had certainly made me see things in a different light. I tried not to dwell on all the complicated personal relationship junk and buried myself in the running of my business. I was doing fairly well, I thought, but then it all went to pot.

"There's a guy in your office, boss," Taylor casually informed me. "He wants to see you right now."

"In my office? Now?"

"Yes, boss."

"How'd he get in there? Who is it?"

"Just go and see. I can handle things out here." Taylor shooed me away and I shook my head.

"Fine, fine, just don't break anything while I'm away."

I ran a mental list of who it could be in the office. No one usually went back there without me, so that list was pretty short. In fact, it basically consisted of two men—two annoying, self-centered, devil-may-care billionaires. My heart raced. I wondered which one it was? I was completely on edge when I opened the door and strode in.

Greg leaned on the edge of my desk, looking down at the tip of his shiny shoe. My heart leaped. My lips suddenly seemed so dry, I had to lick them.

"Oh, hey, did you manage to get hold of Japan then? I imagine it was difficult to get them all in one place at one time." I shut the door behind me and walked toward him with an expansive smile on my face.

"What the fuck is this?" Greg held his lips in a tight line. There wasn't a glimmer of affection to be seen. I looked down to his hand and I already knew what I was going to see there. A newspaper.

"Oh, God," I sighed. "Yeah, Darren helped me out on the bar last night and the pictures got back to the paper. All the rest of the article's utter crap, though."

"Really?" he hissed and slammed the paper down onto the table top. "You really expect me to believe that dickhead Darren just helped out in a menial job to give you a hand? You expect me to swallow that? How stupid do you think I am?"

"I expect you to believe it because it's the truth! He turned up out of the blue, I was short-staffed and he offered to help out, that was it," I yelled back.

"Come on, Kerry, I'm not stupid. Are you going to marry him? Are you going to sell him this place? Fuck, how could you lead me on like this?"

His shoulders slumped and I stretched out to touch him, then as I saw the blazing anger in his eyes I dropped my hand back to my side.

"I haven't led you on. I never said we were exclusive. Yes, I've been seeing Darren but I sure as hell have no plans to marry him and, believe you me, I would never, ever, *ever* sell Diamonds. It's mine and it will always be mine."

"So you slept with Darren last night?" Greg almost whispered the question. He looked to the floor. It was so strange to see him so negative and closed in.

I simply sighed. How could I explain it without making things worse?

"No, don't say anything else, I know all I need to know." Greg pushed away from the desk and moved toward the door.

"Don't leave like this," I pleaded. "Please let me explain—"

"There's nothing to explain, Kerry. I can't do this."

"But it's not what you think, really, it isn't. There's nothing serious between Darren and me but with us..."

I didn't think he'd heard. He'd already walked into the corridor. I waited for a moment, hoping he'd come back, but he didn't. I wanted to chase after him, shout his name and make him come back, but I knew it would be a waste of my time. Greg was gone and I doubted I'd ever see him again.

Back in the bar I continued my shift, numb and unfeeling. I went through the motions. Taylor knew there was something wrong but he didn't ask. I couldn't think, I wouldn't let myself, and on the short

Tube trip home I stared at my phone and played stupid games badly just to avoid the inevitable meltdown I knew was on the way. It didn't work so well since the games were all from Bear Enterprises or Stamford's and each time I saw their logos I choked back a sob of regret.

Still, I held it off fairly well, but as night changed to dawn and I still hadn't closed my eyes I finally let the emotions I was holding in check overwhelm me. I cried, but it felt such a useless thing to do that I dashed the tears from my cheeks and berated myself for being so weak and pathetic. I had to take control of things. Clearly, Greg wasn't happy with me and I wasn't happy with Darren. I had to do something, so I controlled the part of this crazy situation I knew I could.

Exhaling deeply, I picked up my mobile phone. I sent Darren a brief text.

I can't do this anymore. Sorry but I'm calling it off. I've had a great time but I need something more than just sex. I hope you understand. Kerry x

I ummed and ahhed and tossed and turned but finally I sent Greg a text.

I'm sorry. I never meant to hurt you. For the record, I just finished things with Darren. He never made my heart race like you do. Please don't leave it like this. Kerry x

Finally, I found a little rest. I had done all I possibly could.

* * * *

I received a text from Darren that afternoon, questioning the content of my message. I told him I wasn't joking and I really didn't want to hear from him again. I threw myself into work and didn't give it any more thought until later that evening.

"Delivery for you," Martha, one of the waitresses, said as she waltzed past. "Matthew's got it on the door."

"Thanks," I called after her and headed off to the front of the club. Why had a delivery arrived there and so late at night?

When I reached the foyer all became clear. A huge bouquet of flowers lay on the counter. They were from Darren—it said so on the card hidden in the midst of the flowers. I took it off and gave them to Martha.

A huge bunch of similar blooms arrived every day from there on in and every day I gave them to another member of staff. Then the posh boxes of chocolates took over. Those were easy to dole out between us, but when a box containing a diamond-encrusted necklace arrived I texted Darren and told him to stop.

A phone call came through moments later.

"I want you back." Darren didn't even open with a greeting.

"I'm sorry, you can't have me," I replied. I was thoroughly turned off by the whiny note in his voice.

"But, Kerry, we were so good together. You're not with him, are you? You've not chosen Greg over me?" The vehemence in his voice took me back.

"Oh, I should have known. It's all part of the stupid game you two play. You can't bear to lose to him, can you? Well, not that it's any of your business, but I am not yours or his. I am my own woman. Now leave me alone. Stop sending things to the club. I don't want them."

"But—"

"No buts. I don't care how rich you are, pal. You can't buy my love. Goodbye."

I would have slammed down the phone, but it's impossible with a mobile. I just pressed the end call button emphatically and pushed the phone back into my pocket.

Part of me had liked the gifts, the fact that Darren had at least tried to win me back. I'd had nothing from Greg at all. I'd said sorry, I'd hoped he'd at least open some kind of dialog with me, to find out more. I was willing to do whatever it took to get him back but I'd obviously meant even less to him than I'd thought. I'd not even gotten a text.

I was surprised by how much it hurt me. I felt like my heart was breaking, which was daft—we'd not even been in a proper relationship, we'd just been fucking around. Deep inside, in that place we all have where our most essential truths and seediest secrets are hidden, I knew that I was in love with Greg and that I would always be in love with him even if he never spoke to me again. It hurt. I wanted to wallow in self-pity, but I couldn't. I was too busy for a start.

I had gotten one thing from the experience, though. I trusted Taylor with looking after things at work. I regularly got to have a night off and that made me feel better. I loved Diamonds but everyone needed a break to do something different now and then to recharge the batteries.

A few days after the grand break-up over the phone with Darren and thankfully no new presents at work, I took a Sunday off. It was generally a quiet night anyway, when no bank holiday followed, and I found myself at ease knowing my team wouldn't be overwhelmed in my absence.

It was a cold winter's day. The sun never came up, it stayed gray and dull even at noon. I prepared myself a hearty brunch of bacon and eggs and thick sliced toast and tried not to think of a similar dish created for me that morning that seemed a whole lifetime away. I pushed thoughts of Greg from my mind and settled down in front of the TV to veg out and stay warm.

When there was a knock on my door I nearly jumped out of my skin. For a start, people were meant to use the intercom to get in, so I was used to hearing a buzz not a knock. I wondered if it was one of my neighbors, since they'd not needed to use the intercom, but what would they want? I was tempted to ignore the noise but curiosity made me move.

Dragging myself from under my big woollen blanket, I straightened my large baggy jumper and surreptitiously checked for egg stains. I ran fingers through my unbrushed, untamed hair and opened the door.

"Greg?" I gasped. "What are you doing here?"

"Good question," he sighed. "Can I come in and explain?"

I nodded. He looked tired, his shoulders drooped and the skin under his eyes appeared gray, like he'd not been sleeping well.

"I apologize, it's a bit, erm, homely in here." I smoothed down my blanket then picked up my breakfast plate to take into the kitchen. "Would you like a cup of tea?"

"Oh, yes, please," he replied. "I'd love one."

Quickly I disappeared into my little kitchenette and clicked on the kettle. I was very thankful for the comb and mirror I kept there, since every morning I sorted out my hair while I waited for my toast to pop. I couldn't do anything about my clothing, but at least I had gotten dressed today even if it was only in a pair of jogging bottoms and a jumper. I had thought about staying in my PJs all day since I had no plan to see anyone.

I'd been wanting Greg to call so desperately, but what was I going to do with him? What would I say? Could I make things right? I was plagued by questions, including the biggie—why was he here at all?

"Do you take sugar?" I shouted.

"No thanks," he replied. "Just a little milk."

I filled the mugs with tea and gripped their handles. I took a deep breath and walked back into the living room. Greg had straightened out my blanket and smoothed it over the couch like a throw. He'd also picked up the discarded sweet wrappers from beside my chair and placed my part-read book on the coffee table.

"You really would make a great cleaner," I quipped, "if you ever want to start a side business."

"I had to do something to still my nervous energy." He smiled. A little light came to his jaded eyes.

"Well, thank you," I replied, placing his mug on the table before him, and sat next to him on the sofa. I was sure to leave a little space between us. "So what's brought you here?"

"I started out at Diamonds, but you weren't there. I need to talk to you."

Nodding once, I put down my cup before I spilt hot tea all over me. My heart leaped in my chest and I was aware of the blood whizzing through my veins. I was nervous, I didn't know what he'd say next.

"When I saw that picture on the front of that horrid rag I was enraged. I couldn't believe you'd be so pally with him. I knew deep down that the write-up was journalistic crap, but the idea of you and him going into business together or, worse still, marrying made me so angry I couldn't think straight. I didn't give you time to explain, I didn't want to. I wanted to put an end to it all. I couldn't afford to give you a second chance. I wasn't sure I could trust you. But, and I am so scared of telling you this"—he paused, exhaled noisily and ran a hand through his thick, dark hair—"I couldn't stop thinking about you. Every night before I sleep I see your face and you're on my mind when I wake up. I haven't been able to forget you. In fact, as time has gone on I've missed you more and more. I've become more restless, I've not been able to concentrate at all. I've never felt like this about a woman before."

Greg glanced back up at me then directed his gaze to the floor again. I wanted him to continue, to clarify what I thought he was telling me.

"So I had to come and see you. I'm absolutely petrified that you're going to tell me to piss off and leave you alone but I have to tell you this. I *have* to tell you this." He took a breath. I held mine.

"I think I might love you, Kerry."

Stunned, I said nothing at first then he looked up at me and he looked so tortured, so scared that I had to reach out and cup his cheek. I felt the prickly stubble there. He'd not shaved in a while. I leaned in and kissed him. I kissed him hard and deep and I hoped my answer came through in the passion of my assault.

"I was terrified you'd reject me, or you'd be engaged to— Well, I'm not going to mention his name," he said when we took breath. I hugged him tightly and kissed the curve of his neck. "I am *so* sorry, Kerry."

"Sorry? Why sorry?"

"Because I didn't treat you right before. I wasn't good enough for you."

"No," I shook my head. "No, you were a perfect gentleman." I sat back and took his hands in mine. "I had a fantastic time with you, I really did. I should have been totally upfront with you, and I was the one who ruined everything, but to put your mind at rest, I finished things with Darren. He wasn't the man I wanted."

Greg let out a shuddering breath. "You don't know how relieved I am to hear you say that. I was dreading you telling me you were in love with him."

"No." I shook my head. "No, I'm not in love with him. I think I'm in love with you. I've not been able to get you out of my mind. It really hurt that you didn't try to communicate with me. I thought I'd completely blown it, I've been heartbroken."

"I should have done this earlier," Greg pulled his hands from under mine and wrapped me in an embrace. "I'm just a stupid man with a big ego who doesn't know how to love."

"Maybe we can learn together?"

"Sounds good to me," he said. "Now kiss me, please kiss me, I need you."

So I did and it felt like it marked the beginning of the rest of our lives together. It was the perfect way to start, lip to lip and heart to heart with a man I could discover love with.

"I've missed you so much," he whispered, his breath caressing my ear as his big, familiar hands captured my hips.

"I've missed you too." I worked on the buttons on the front of his shirt. "You've been constantly in my thoughts, I've not been able to think straight."

"I should be in New York right now," he replied, shrugging the material from his shoulders then pulling up my jumper, revealing my lack of bra beneath, "but I sent someone else instead. I couldn't bear being without you for even a moment longer."

He kissed my neck and I curled my arms around him, reveled in the heat of his body against mine. "I'm so glad you came. You won't get into trouble for missing your meeting, though, will you?"

"I'm the billionaire boss, sweetheart. I hand out trouble, I don't get any back. Well, apart from off you. You seem to have a knack for it."

"Trouble? Me?" I attempted my best innocent look. Greg laughed, the joyful sound prompting my own giggles.

"Yes, you. I should spank you for all the heartache you've caused me."

"Oh, please do." I bit my lip but the brazen words had escaped before I'd really had time to think about them.

"Cheeky madam," he exclaimed then sat back on the sofa behind him. After making himself comfortable he patted his lap.

I gulped, danced from foot to foot, and as his stern gaze burned through my resistance I sank down over his lap, fingertips touching the floor one side, my toes the other.

"I have dreamed about this so many times," he cooed and pulled down my tracksuit bottoms and gave me a light opening slap. "Your arse is fucking perfection, especially once I get a little flush of pink on it." He stroked my bum lovingly and I really felt cherished. Tears pricked behind my eyes, not with pain but with joy.

He continued the spanks. Rhythmically he increased the force behind each hit until I was squirming in a genuine bid to get away. It really hurt and I sobbed as the tears continued to fall down my cheeks. It might sound like he was abusing me to someone who didn't understand the way I worked, but he wasn't. I really needed it. Greg had aroused this need in me, something I hadn't realized was missing before I met him. I found the freedom to cry and let go of all the negativity that had built up inside was incredibly freeing. As the tears dripped, I felt the weight of sorrow within me lessen. On top of that emotional release, I needed the physical pain, because not only was it retribution for my stupidity, it also marked me as his and I wanted that. I wanted to wear my spanked red cheeks like a label proclaiming him to be my master.

"Now that's perfection." Greg traced his fingertips over my stinging cheeks, trailing tingles of sharp pain beneath his stubby nails. "And my, you are a naughty, naughty girl," he continued as he slid his fingers into the heat between my legs. "You're so fucking wet."

He slowly inserted a finger into me then when he drew it out he added more digits and slammed them back inside, stretching me and making a rude, squelching noise as my juices clung to his thrusting fingers.

Pleasure pumped through me in time with his powerful thrusts. I could feel an orgasm building and I was so close to tumbling over into ecstasy when he withdrew his fingers completely.

"Stand up," he commanded. "I'm going to fuck you now."

I scrambled up off his knees and waited for him to join me. He grabbed my hand and pulled me into the bedroom. I cringed at the sight of my unmade bed, but he just tossed the duvet to the floor then started to undo his trousers.

I clambered onto the bed, eager to feel him inside me. I lay back and traced my fingers lazily over my breasts as I watched him shed his clothes.

"Condom?" His tone conveyed the question and I nodded to the decorative box on the table beside the bed. He opened it up and took out a package and jumped onto the bed beside me. I rolled to my side and caressed his chest. He crinkled and crumpled the packet and pulled out its contents.

I watched him sheathe himself and continued to trace my fingertips across his flesh. When the condom was seated properly I climbed to my knees and he pulled me over him until I straddled his waist. He guided me down onto his cock with one hand on my hip and the other on his erection, guiding it between my wet lips.

I closed my eyes and enjoyed the stretch of him inside me. I'd thought I'd never see him again, never feel him again. I wanted to remember every moment of this coupling—it was going to be the beginning of something special.

"Oh, Kerry," he groaned, and when I opened my eyes I saw him gazing up at me. "I love you," he continued and I could see the spark of vulnerability in his eyes and that struck a chord within me.

"I love you too, Greg, I love you too," I chanted. "I'm so sorry."

"Sh." He lifted his finger and pressed it to my lips. "You don't need to say it, we don't want to dwell on it. We're here now together, and I want to be with you forever, that's all that matters."

"Yes," I agreed, the friction of his cock inside me and the deep meaning of his words making my insides tremor in bliss. "Oh fuck, yes. Don't ever leave me, Greg, please. Never leave me."

"I never will," he gasped, gripping my hip tighter with one hand and dropping the other to where we were joined. He pressed against my clit and with a few more thrusts I came. Hard and fast and with such passion that I cried out loudly and curled up around him. He grabbed both hips and drove into my replete body, slamming into me until his own orgasm sparked. He called my name and pulled me down to his chest. He cradled me in his arms as we panted out the lingering throb of pleasure and rode on the euphoria of contentment.

Sliding to lie beside him I found myself cradled in his arm, my head in the nook of Greg's shoulder. My buttocks stung and the rest of me was relaxed in mellow repletion.

"Are you busy tomorrow?" Greg asked, rousing me from my journey to sleep.

"Hmm, well, I should be at the club, but Taylor's getting good at managing in my absence."

"How do you fancy flying with me into the sunset?"

"Where will we go?"

"Wherever you like."

"I've always fancied Venice."

"Then we shall go to Venice. Book the rest of the week off work. I'll go and ring Chester and set it all up."

"Okay."

I rolled out of bed and started to pack.

Chapter Seven

It was the moment I stepped into the water taxi that it truly hit home that we were in Venice. Water surrounded us, the airport loomed behind and I followed Greg onto a small, dark wood boat that looked like something straight out of a James Bond film. He held my hand as I delicately made my way down the steps.

"*Ca de Conti, per favore*," Greg confidently spoke to the taxi driver. I wondered for a moment if he actually was a driver, considering his taxi floated. Did that make him a taxi captain?

"Is that man a taxi driver, sailor or captain?" I asked when Greg came to join me in the seated area behind the man in charge of the vehicle. He sat on the plump leather sofa directly beside me even though there was room for a dozen people in the cabin at least.

"I don't know," Greg replied. "I've never thought about that." He wrapped an arm around my shoulders. "And to be truthful, I'm not thinking about that right now, either."

The engine purred to life, the blue water stirred around us and the boat moved forward.

"What are you thinking?" I asked, directing my question to the curve of his ear, tempted to lean in and nibble his lobe, it looked so inviting.

"I was thinking it'd be hot to fuck you in a water taxi."

My breath caught in my throat and was kept there as Greg captured my lips with his. He ran his hand down my arm and clasped my hand. He gently tugged until my palm cupped his crotch and I could feel the erection straining against the material. The warm air stirred through my hair, I could smell the water and feel the heat on my face from the sun shining through the glass. He finally pulled back so I could breathe.

"But we'll be seen," I gasped.

"Our captain is occupied," he said, "and if I push you down here"—he shoved me and I sprawled out on the long, blue chair, the cold leather cooling my heated skin—"no one else will be able to see."

He quickly climbed above me, slipping his legs between mine. I strained my neck to look behind me. The swarthy gentleman who we'd decided to call captain was definitely absorbed in looking forward, not back, and although I could see the sky above us, I could no longer see any of the other vessels crowding the busy waterway. My heart thudded in my chest.

Greg leaned on one arm and ran the other hand down over my hip to the edge of my short, flippy skirt. He pushed it up and wiggled his fingers against the crotch of my knickers.

"You're soaked," he groaned, rubbing his fingers up, over and around my tingling clit. "You want this as much as I do."

His hard gaze never left mine. His pupils were so wide with lust that his eyes seemed ebony black. I fell into the depths of them and just nodded.

He gripped the crotch of my knickers and pulled it to the side. His trousers were already loosened I noticed, as I gazed down his body to see his long erection open to the air.

"Shit, condom," he cursed and paused in his movements.

"I'm on the pill," I gulped. "I've never fucked a guy without a condom before."

"I've never fucked without a condom either," he replied, gaze locked with mine. "I really want you, but I'll wait if you need the extra protection…"

"No"—after only a second's hesitation—"I trust you, Greg. Just fuck me, please."

Greg looked up, checking on the captain I presumed, then he looked down at me with a broad grin.

"My first," he whispered, shuffling forward and pressing his cock down to rub against my wet slit.

My eyes brimmed with tears at the soft, tender words and the significance of the moment. His eyes closed, he slid inside me and I couldn't keep mine open either as the spark of lust ignited. He pushed his way gently into me. My walls eased wide for him then clutched him tightly. I reveled in the warmth of his flesh against my flesh, the intimacy of the act.

Greg curled his body over me and I wrapped my ankles around his back and held him tight, only momentarily wondering if my ankles would be on view to the boats around. It would be very obvious what we were up to if all they could see were my linked ankles. However, I didn't care. The man I loved was inside me, hard, hot and unsheathed. We were sharing a first together and I was overwhelmed by the strength of love that flowed between us.

The coupling was short and fast. He came inside me and I clung to him, ankles and hands linked around his body, holding him tight. Our eyes opened and we kissed. Smiles blossomed across our faces then Greg quickly scrambled back, zipped himself up and sat prim and proper in his seat. I followed him and a moment later we were snuggled together in a polite embrace. Only the flush of red in his cheeks and mine — I knew they were, I could feel the heat — even hinted at what had happened seconds before.

"We are here." The captain finally looked over his shoulder as he cut the engine.

"Thank you." Greg stood and offered me his hand. He led me off the boat and directly into the hotel. The big black doors in their white stone frame opened directly out onto the canal. Greg handed over payment then followed me into the marble grandeur of the hotel reception.

You would think that after a while you'd get used to being surrounded by opulence. I can tell you that I was as awed in that hotel as I had been in London and in Paris. Everywhere sparkled. It smelled fresh and floral. There was marble and gold leaf and big mirrors. I felt like I'd stepped back in time.

Greg dealt with the receptionist in Italian. I had no idea what he said but it was intensely sexy to hear him speaking in a foreign tongue. We were guided up a few flights of stairs and to a huge white door. Greg palmed a tip to the young lad and he smiled, nodded and headed back down the stairs when Greg pushed open the door and stepped back to let me go first.

I was expecting to see just a room with a bed — naïve, I know, but I hadn't been in the company of a billionaire long enough to expect anything more. The room I entered was huge, with blue walls flecked with ornate gold diamonds and furniture that looked like it belonged in a museum. But there were stairs in the room, leading up. I had to follow them.

They curved round and ended on a mezzanine floor. Before me was a huge bed, bedecked in blue silks and swaged with gold drapes. The rest of the room was decorated with just a few modest pieces of dark, curvaceously lined furniture. It was stunningly beautiful.

"Eighteenth-century elegance, you can't beat it." Greg wrapped a strong arm around my waist and rested his chin on my shoulder.

"I feel like a princess," I sighed happily. "Like a fairy story come to life."

"Oh no, sweetheart, that will be tomorrow night. It's Carnival time here in Venice and I have an invite to the best masquerade ball in town."

"Really?" My voice took on a high-pitched squeak. "I've always wanted to go to a masquerade ball."

"Really. And we'll go shopping for costumes tomorrow."

"And we'll get masks?" I barely contained my excitement.

"Yes," he purred. "I'll buy you a mask."

"I can afford to buy my own mask, you know." I bristled, my mind cast back to a similar conversation with Darren.

"I know, sweetheart, but let me spoil you. I've missed you so much." He spun me round until I faced him.

I was about to argue with him that money and gifts couldn't make up for lost time, but he bent his head and kissed me and I lost track of my argument. I was still fizzing with sexual energy from the encounter on the canal and so I easily gave up my high ground to be pushed gently but inexorably toward the bed. I might be a strong independent woman, but come on, who didn't like to be spoiled every now and then?

"You're so soft," he groaned in my ear. He stretched beside me and slid his hand up my thigh. "And giving. And so damn sexy."

Greg leaned over and kissed me and all protest—all thought, come to that—disappeared from my mind. He continued to insinuate his hand farther under my skirt, pushing up and under the light floral cotton until the tips of his fingers brushed the sodden material of my knickers. He growled his approval. His lips never left mine as he scrambled his fingers under the fabric and onto my springy pubic hair.

My hips lifted and pushed against him in a wanton display of need and lust. I bumped my hips and when I wriggled he moved his touch lower until one of his long fingers ran down the length of my sodden slit. He moved one way as I bounced the other and I was soon panting and moaning against his lips as a powerful orgasm stirred deep within me. He didn't stop, he didn't tease me. I think he knew how desperate I was for release.

Snippets of our escapade in the water taxi came back to me as my clit tingled from his strokes. The ruffle of the breeze on my bare legs, the cold leather that warmed against my back, the drone of the motor, the thrill of being seconds away from discovery. All that coalesced with the attention Greg lavished upon me and I came. My hips lifted up off the bed and my lips pressed hard and tight against his.

"For the record," I gasped and snuggled into his body, "that will not always be the best way to stop an argument between us."

Greg kissed the top of my head and I snuggled into him. "I know." He stroked my upper arm. "But it's a pretty good weapon to have in my arsenal."

I chuckled, content to rest against him and let the rhythm of my heart slow. I knew he wasn't trying to buy my affection so I let the matter rest and I drifted off to sleep in the shelter of his arms.

We woke up a little later and went out to explore. It was wonderful to be in a place of such beauty with the man I loved. It was also quiet. The media hadn't gotten wind of his trip.

"I'm sure they'll find me eventually. They always do," Greg replied when I pointed out the lack of cameras pointing at him. "But it's good to have a break from them."

"I bet. I'm not sure I could do it."

"Well, darling, if you're going to spend much time with me, you'll have to get used to it."

"For you" — I stopped walking and turned to him — "I could learn to put up with anything."

"Anything?" he growled and cocked his head to the side.

"Uh-huh," I whispered, tipping my head back and kissing him. The world passed on by as we embraced. I didn't care who watched, I was lost in his kiss.

"I will remember that." He smiled. "And maybe I'll hold you to it."

"I hope so." I dropped my gaze to my shoe tips and we continued to meander along the winding streets of Venice. We ended up at the Ponte della Paglia and gazed at the famed Bridge of Sighs.

"I've always wanted to see this place since I heard about it as a child. I don't know why, the legend with it about the prisoners is such a morbid one."

"Ah, but have you heard of another legend, one far lighter and much more romantic?"

"No." I shook my head.

"Well, the sun is going down and I know where we can hire a gondola. When we're on the boat I will tell you it."

I'd not been on a boat in years before Venice. It had only been one of those pedal boats when I had been young and Richard Parks from the year below me in school had been trying to win me over. Making me get in a cold plastic boat on a typically wet British summertime day then making me pedal to move the silly-looking swan hadn't worked to his advantage.

The gondola I got into with Greg was a far grander affair with red velvet seats, the back in the shape of a heart, surrounded with ornate golden twists of foliage and decorated with peachy-bottomed cherubs. Greg gave his instructions to the striped-topped gondolier in Italian then settled in his seat beside me, clasping my hand in his.

"I'm intensely impressed by your Italian, love," I purred.

"Why, thank you." He leaned in and kissed my cheek. "I speak it fairly well, along with a few other languages."

"What else do you speak?"

"Limited Japanese and Chinese, some Spanish, then I'm fairly accomplished at German and French. I've always loved languages. I also find people are happier to do business with you if you can talk to them in their own language, or you at least give it a try."

"Top tip." I nodded. "And very impressive."

"Yes," he whispered, his lips set close to my ear so the man behind couldn't hear. "I can ask you to fuck me in several different languages."

My cheeks flushed with heat and I hoped the gondolier was too busy maneuvering us from the dock to have overheard.

"Anyway, back to the topic at hand." He leaned back and I composed myself, though the heat of passion still flowed in my veins. "The other legend of the Bridge of Sighs is so much lovelier and it's why this good man is directing us toward it now."

The boat bobbed gently in the water, the long prow splitting it in front of us, and the muscle and pole of the gondolier pushed us forward at a sedate pace. The golden orb of the sun sank over the city and daubed the white walls with oranges and warm yellows. The Bridge of Sighs before us seemed to shine in the light, the corridor of buildings leading us toward the halo that hung so far above the blue canal.

"Local legend has it" — Greg turned toward me as we approached the bridge — "that if a couple kiss in a gondola under the Bridge of Sighs at sunset then their love will last forever."

I beamed at him, the soft light of sunset bathed us and, as the shadow of the famous bridge covered us, his lips pressed against mine. It felt like magic, the golden sun like fire around us, the shadow of the bridge holding us, the sound of the water and the peace of that moment. I wanted the legend to be true. I'd not even thought about forever with Greg but when he kissed me it became a dream I wanted to achieve.

He pulled back, stroking his hand gently down my arm and smiling, a little hesitantly, a tad unsure. I reached out a hand and cupped his face, wanting to reassure him to make him feel better.

"That's you and me bound forever then," I said with a lighthearted giggle. "I hope you're ready for it."

He nodded and turned his head to kiss the inside of my hand.

"I think I can work with that," he murmured, "you in bondage to me forever."

Trust him to twist the romance into something kinky and sexual. Or maybe that was just me, maybe it was what I hoped he meant. I wanted him to tie me down and use me—but maybe not right there, under the nose of a poor working man and half of Venice who'd come out to see the Bridge of Sighs at the most romantic time of the day.

It was later that night that he showed me the meaning of his kinky words. We'd enjoyed a meal in our room. Greg was hoping to keep a low profile for as long as possible.

"We were just out on the canal below the Bridge of Sighs where a lot of people saw us, Greg, I'm not sure that's keeping a low profile."

"No," he replied, "you can't let the possibility of discovery get in the way of good romance. And if a tourist snapped us? Well, it will take time for them to contact the media and get those photos circulated. It's not like I kissed you in front of a horde of paparazzi."

"I'll give you that," I conceded, hoping my thoughtless answer wouldn't leave him in a bad mood all evening.

"And you'll give me more." He didn't smile. His face was stony lined and I really didn't know what he would do next. "Go and stand at the bottom of the stairs."

I was about to argue, I must admit. I wasn't going to be commanded about like a naughty child. Greg leaned in and whispered in my ear.

"I want to have some fun. Play along, please. If you want to stop just shout 'Diamonds', okay?"

I nodded tersely and went to stand just before the first stair that led up to the mezzanine floor. I looked around, unsure of what to do. I felt a little silly stood there, waiting for something to happen.

"I've been looking at this staircase since we arrived, imagining you bent over, holding onto the spindles and waiting for a damn good spanking. Hold onto the rails and bend over, my dream's about to come true."

I gulped and licked my lips. The image now danced in my mind too. I turned round, swung around the last post and readied myself by bending and gripping two rails in front of me.

"Oh yeah, that's it," he moaned. I glanced to the left and saw him walking toward me, his jaw set determinedly. My knees buckled beneath me. I don't know what the medical diagnosis for it would have been but I guessed it was because all my blood had drained down to the lower parts of my body and left my brain high and dry.

I gripped the cold, hard beams all the tighter and was grateful to feel his hands on my hips to help hold me up. I was even more grateful to feel him hitch up my skirt and fold it over my back until my rump was revealed, the light lace of my knickers the only thing that protected my modesty.

A rumble of appreciation rolled from his lips and vibrated through his body until I felt it transfer from his hands into me. I melted under his touch. Even when he lifted a hand and let it drop hard onto my arse I tightened up but I didn't want him to stop. I wanted the delicious pain to continue. He read my mind as his slaps rained down rhythmically. Each impact shook me, pushed arousal through my body and as my buttocks stung, ecstasy blossomed. My nipples peaked and rubbed painfully against my bra, my clit plumped, my pussy moistened until the strip of lace covering me was soaked, the material clung to my lips.

"So pretty and pink, but this is in the way," Greg peeled down my knickers, let them drop to the floor in a flutter of freedom. "Oh, much better."

He stroked my buttocks, the sting revived with his touch. I was torn. I wanted more punishment but I also wanted release.

He gripped my hips tightly and pressed his crotch against me, his trouser-covered cock nestling between my buttocks.

I rubbed back against him, desperate for more of him. I bent my legs and straightened them again as I communicated my lust to Greg, desperate for him to give me more but with desire so great words wouldn't come.

He stepped back and I heard the clunk of his belt being unfastened and the hiss of the dropped zip. The next time I felt his pressure on me it was from his naked cock probing between my buttocks. He bent his legs and maneuvered around me, using a hand to press his erection into my wet slit and the other to grip my hip. Once he filled me he held onto me with both hands and thrust hard.

I braced myself, tried to hold it together when pain and pleasure at each impact mixed and coalesced, taking my breath away. He slammed hard and fast and he came inside me after just a few moments. The deep-seated grunt he made flooded me with second-hand satisfaction. I didn't have time to think—he pulled out, dragged me up and turned me around in his arms. He pressed my back against the banisters. He sought out my slit with probing fingers and slid up and down to find my clit. We kissed, mouths mashed together between gasps and pants. I was pure, writhing need and when I came, I screamed against his lips and the pleasure ripped from me, intense and immense.

He held me up, breath tickling my cheek.

"That was better than I imagined," Greg whispered. "You're amazing, Kerry."

"So are you," I sighed. "Now I think I need to lie down, my knees have forgotten what they're meant to be doing."

We giggled up the stairs and into the luxurious bed, throwing our remaining clothes off as we went. I snuggled into his shoulder and was just nodding off when I heard the strains of a song, a ringtone. I thought I was dreaming, but Greg cursed and leaped from the bed. He hurtled downstairs and a moment later he snapped out a greeting.

I didn't get the content of the rest of the conversation. Just that Greg was pissed off at being contacted but that the issue at hand was one of major importance. A few moments later he was back at my side.

"I'm sorry, I'm going to have to go and do some work. I'll take the laptop down into one of the quieter communal areas so I don't disturb you. I've got more employees to yell at before the night is through."

"Oh, okay," I mumbled, disappointed to not have him in bed with me but too tired to argue.

"I'll miss you," he sighed and bent to kiss me.

"I'll miss you too, sweetheart. Don't work too hard."

He picked up his clothes and walked back down the stairs at a much more sedate pace. I heard him sigh once more then the door closed behind him. I wondered if our relationship would always be just the bits between our jobs.

It struck me as weird that I was bothered by that idea. I was a career girl myself and would put my job before almost everything else. I was surprised to realize that I wouldn't put work in front of him. I'd drop anything at a moment's notice. I could even imagine selling Diamonds to be with him full-time. I'd never even contemplated that in theory before.

Would Greg do the same for me? Big questions plagued me and prevented me from falling into the satisfied sleep I'd been heading for. I tossed and turned for a while until the softness of the bed and the lateness of the hour finally won over and I slept. My mind, however, was busy with upsetting dreams.

Chapter Eight

"I know it's late, Stephano, but all this happened at the last minute. Surely you've got something for us."

Greg had climbed into bed with me sometime in the early hours. I had woken much earlier than him, gone for a walk and enjoyed breakfast at a sweet little corner café. I'd wished Greg could have been with me but I understood he needed to sleep, so I'd left him to it. He had still been asleep when I'd gotten back at lunchtime but he'd woken not long after and whisked me off to a very exclusive designer shop. I'd been a bit disappointed that we hadn't indulged in anything intimate before we'd left.

"I do not like having to dress you and your beautiful partner with what I have lying about. You need shaping and molding. I mean, look at her hips. Oh, the joy I could get from draping them properly with cloth." Stephano ran me over with his professional gaze. It heated my blood. He was a good-looking fellow, hard lines and with just a little stubble on his chin. The impeccably cut suit emphasized his length and his litheness. If it was one of his own it was a great advertisement for his skills.

"I know, I know, but come on, you must have *something*." Greg didn't quite flutter his lashes but he wasn't far off — it was arousing to watch him in action. No wonder he was so successful — Greg wasn't going to back down.

"Come, come, we will see." Stephano walked off and we trailed behind. Greg grabbed my hand and squeezed it.

"Okay, so with your dark hair and your light skin, *signora*, I believe this rich blue will complement you most pleasantly." Stephano indicated a dress on a mannequin in front of him. It was stunning. The color reminded me of peacocks. The material was obviously rich — silk, I suspected.

"Wow," I gasped, unable to vocalise anything else.

"I think she likes it," Greg beamed.

"*Bellissimo.*" Stephano clapped his hands together and a young lady appeared from somewhere in the back. "Juliet, remove this gown from display and prepare it to be tried on." She went about her task efficiently and Stephano moved over to a rack of jackets.

"We have this in the same color set. It is the same period, eighteenth century, and I think it will suit you well, *Signore* Stamford."

The jacket was stunning, long and shaped to the waist in a similar shimmering blue fabric with gold brocade and golden buttons along its length. "So smart," I squealed and Greg nodded.

Stephano beamed proudly. "I believe we have some breeches that will match well enough and we have shirts. I think we may just be able to pull this off."

Stephano pulled Greg off into a changing room on one side of the huge room and Juliet ushered me into one on the opposite side. I felt a little uncomfortable because she stayed with me while I took off my clothes. The room was the size of three or four of the small booths you get in department stores, so at least it did not feel quite so intimate, but I was not used to stripping off layers in front of a stranger. Juliet, however, did her best to put me at ease.

I stood before her in my lingerie and she smiled encouragingly. I felt silly. I wanted to cover my stomach and thighs, I felt so big in comparison to her. She was slim and trim. I imagined what she was thinking of me and none of it was pleasant.

"So we shall go into the dress, yes?" She smiled and held the back of the huge confection of expensive material open for me to step into.

"Okay." I stepped forward and into the layers and Juliet arranged them around me.

"I wish I had your figure," she sighed and strapped me in. "I have no hips."

"You can have some of mine if you like," I responded with a surprised smile, "but you are gorgeous just as you are."

"*Grazie*, you are too kind, *signora*."

"Well, it's true," I continued. "You've got to embrace what you've been given." As the words fell from my lips I realized that I should take my own advice.

Juliet blushed and brushed the dress around me. It fitted surprisingly well. I was used to settling for clothing that fitted adequately—I was tall and generously curved, so it was hard to find anything in the shops that catered for my curves and my height. This gown in all its historical glory cupped me gently but firmly. My breasts peeped from the top of the gentle white lace and my hips were nestled in the soft silk and satin of the underskirts. My waist seemed to have magically shrunk. The image of me in the mirror had to be a fairy tale.

I was in the center of layers of skirts. I could feel their weight, but it wasn't too uncomfortable. I admired the delicate embroidery on the bodice of my dress, long rows of golden embroidered flowers, with pearls and sequins sparkling and highlighting the delicate work that rolled down onto the body of the skirts. The middle panel was edged with golden brocade, separating it from the plain silk of the outer areas of the gown.

Juliet pressed my hand into a sleeve and I let her pull a long lined jacket over my arms. I gasped when she pulled it over my other shoulder and moved round me to straighten the velvet frock coat. The dark softness caressed my curves, and the softly rounded and shaped edges revealed the light eggshell blue silk of the lining and the golden brocade and sparkling sequins that lay there.

"You like?" Juliet asked after a few moments of me staring at my reflection in the mirror.

I just nodded. Tears pricked at my eyes. I looked like a princess, like I'd walked out of the history books. I couldn't believe how emotional I felt simply because of a dress. Juliet squeezed my shoulder and smiled.

"Many women react the same," she said. "It is a revelation, yes?"

"Oh, yes," I replied with a nod. "Can I show Greg?"

"Yes, yes. I shall go and see if they are ready."

Juliet bustled out of the changing room and I tried swishing my dress from side to side. It moved with such ease that I giggled with joy and stepped back then forward to watch the material move and settle around me. It was stunning.

"Come, *signora*, your prince, he awaits."

I felt so light and happy as I walked out into that shop. I know it sounds shallow, some pretty clothes made me feel good, but they did. I can't deny it. I knew it wasn't long-lasting, I knew it wasn't a turning point in my life, but I felt good and I reveled in it.

I gawped at Greg waiting there for me. He was a prince. The tight blue breeches clung to his legs above the startling white stockings and matching blue shoes. That long coat we'd viewed earlier clung to his broad shoulders and cascaded down his lithe body to emphasize his manliness. The matching waistcoat below held tight to his chest, the bright white of a ruffled shirt below it, showing off the deepness of his tan.

Greg looked me over as I took him in. Our gazes met and we laughed, the joy and craziness of the situation spilling out from our lips.

"You look stunning," he said and walked toward me.

"You too," I replied, reaching out to stroke the soft material of his jacket.

"You both like?" Stephano's voice broke into our moment and we looked up at the designer. I nodded and Greg answered for us.

"We love them, Stephano. They're perfect."

I was very reluctant to take the robe off again but I had to. We had the masks still to buy. When I emerged in my boring long dress and cardigan, Greg was taking back his credit card from the smiling Stephano.

"I shall send them over now, *signore*, so they will await you at the hotel."

"Wonderful, thank you."

Greg waved at me when I walked over then slipped his arm around my waist. "Ready to go mask shopping, my princess?" I nodded, my cheeks flushed from his compliment and touch.

We'd not walked far before we were faced by a man with a large camera. It was immediately apparent he was interested in taking photos of us, not the pretty town around us.

"Well, I knew they'd find me eventually." Greg shrugged and we continued walking. I didn't think I could ever be so dismissive of being photographed. I supposed that you got used to it in time, and Greg must have had journalists poking into his business for many years—he had started his computer company in his late teens and had been in the media ever since.

The shop we went to had windows filled with masks of all shapes and sizes. It was clear what its business was. We went in and I wondered if we'd ever find what we wanted—there were just so many different masks to choose from. Large ones, small ones, ones to cover the whole face, eye masks, ones on sticks and ones with huge, long noses.

Greg was talking to a short man in an apron. I was sure the apron had once been white, but years of wear and paint splatters meant it was far more colorful than its original state. He nodded and pointed out a mask. Greg took it down off the wall and held it out to me. It was perfect.

"This is a columbina mask," Greg told me. "It's easier on the wearer as it leaves half the face uncovered."

"It's beautiful," I gasped and traced the gold brocade around the edge with my finger. The mask was delicate and light when I took it from his hands and the gold glitter sparkled when I tipped it from side to side. The bright blue ribbons tickled my wrists and I imagined they'd be soft against my skin when I tied it on. The painting around the cheeks and over the bridge of the nose was delicate and exquisite, small flowers and leaves twirled together in all the shades of blue featured in my dress, picked out by the golden highlights. It was as if the mask had been made to complement my outfit.

"Do you like it?" Greg asked.

"Oh, yes, I love it. It's perfect," I gushed.

"Then that one is yours. Now we just need to pick one out for me. *Signore*?" He turned to the shopkeeper, who looked at the mask in my hand, bit his brown, wrinkled lip in contemplation then strode past us with great purpose.

I gazed around me and was lost in my surroundings, so Greg grabbed my elbow and led me along. It was a strange mix of joyful and creepy being surrounded by so many bright colors, sequins and sparkles and so many empty, staring eye sockets.

"How is this one?" The shop owner spoke in a deeply accented tone. He passed Greg a mask in a similar style to mine, but the feminine frills and flowers were replaced by a highly sheened dark blue luster and one single three-feathered decoration at the middle of the forehead, one single golden jewel directly in the center of the plume.

"What do you think?" Greg held it up before his eyes and I nodded emphatically.

"Oh yes, that's very you," I said. "Very masculine, it'll go perfectly with your outfit."

"Brilliant," he replied, leaning in to gently kiss my lips. I felt embarrassed—the poor shopkeeper didn't need to see such an intimate gesture. He didn't seem to be bothered about it, though. He was already striding off toward the till.

After paying, Greg looked at his watch as our masks were wrapped in layers of tissue paper.

"Well, we've managed that just in the nick of time." He laughed. "Just time to get back and get changed, I think."

It was a short walk back to the hotel. We strolled along hand in hand. Greg carried the paper bag with our masks in and it swung at his side with each step. I was happy in his presence. The questions that had plagued me the night before seemed silly in the light of day with his hand in mine.

The sun was dropping when we came up to the hotel front. It glinted off the water of the canal and warmed the white bricks around us to burnished orange. I thought it was busy but thought nothing more of it until the crowd of people surged toward us and the noise and flashes of cameras brought me to the realization of what was going on.

"Keep your head down. Say nothing," Greg whispered in my ear and gripped my hand all the tighter.

"Are you on holiday, Mr Stamford?"

"Why are you here with Darren Bennett's girlfriend?"

I went to snap at the man asking such a rude question but Greg squeezed my hand and pulled me back, so I stopped.

"Miss Matthews, are you playing the field?"

"Are you not marrying Darren Bennett?"

"Who is looking after your club?"

The questions came thick and fast as we bowed our heads and pushed through the crowd and into the foyer of the Ca Dei Conte where the doormen stopped the yammering journalists in their tracks.

"I'm so sorry," Greg sighed.

"It's not your fault," I responded, squeezing his hand. "Don't worry about it."

"It's not pleasant." He shrugged. "But sadly it's part of my life."

"Well, I want to be part of your life so I'll have to get used to it."

Greg stopped at the bottom of the staircase and kissed me.

"Thank you," he whispered then pulled me up the stairs after him. "I am so glad you're in my life, Kerry. I don't know what I'd do without you."

In the room we got down to it—getting dressed to go to the ball. After I showered and tried to tame my curls into something sedate and elegant, Greg helped me into my gown. The moment I pressed myself into its comforting, soft folds I felt better. I was instantly an elegant lady without a worry in the world. I slipped my feet into the soft blue slippers we'd bought to match my outfit and fussed and faffed as Greg dressed himself.

"My lady." He held out my mask. "Let me assist you."

"Why, thank you, kind sir."

Greg walked behind me and lowered the mask over my face from above. I guided it into position onto my nose and Greg smoothed his hand along the sides, over my ears, and grasped the ties to pull and fasten the ribbons behind my head. I felt constricted but not painfully so. It was exciting to be covered and disguised from the world—I could do anything I wanted, or so I felt.

I helped Greg into his mask and ran my fingers through his hair as I tied him in. He carried the ensemble off perfectly. He held himself tall and proud and where I imagined some men would look comical covered in such bright colors and curls, he looked confident and hot.

We shared a be-masked kiss. On the second attempt we managed it without cracking our hard noses together. His lips were hot and giving and all I wanted was for him to strip all those clothes off again, even though it'd taken such time to get ready — I forgot all that at the press of his lips against mine.

"We'd best go, Kerry. It's getting late and if I kiss you again we're not going to leave this room tonight."

"Would that be such a bad thing?"

"No," he admitted and pulled his body from mine, "but there are three good reasons for going. One, I don't like to waste good money, two, I want to walk into the party with the most beautiful woman on my arm, and three, the Conte would kill me if I didn't turn up to his party after I went to such lengths to get invited."

"Fair enough," I shrugged. "I can wait."

"I can too," he replied and licked his lips. "Just."

It was a little easier to ignore the journalists on our way out, since we stepped straight from the hotel into a waiting water taxi. The flashes were blinding from all the cameras pointed our way. I just smiled and hoped I looked good on the photos. I was sure I would, I was dressed in such wonderful clothes.

I stepped gingerly down into the body of the boat and swept my dress down before sitting.

"I'm glad I don't have to wear this every day," I sighed. "It would get wearying, I'm sure."

"I don't think I could do business in these breeches," Greg replied. "I don't think my rivals would take me seriously."

We laughed and as the bright lights and chattering of the paparazzi were left behind us we continued to chat and get back into the party frame of mind.

The Conte's home was directly connected to the canal. It wasn't a particularly ornate building, made of the white stone that dominated Venice and relatively plain in its exterior. Inside, however, was a revelation. It was precisely like I'd stepped back in time—the rooms were immaculate, high-ceilinged and covered with plaster relief work, ornate and gold-leafed.

We were led by a liveried young man through a vaulted hall, past an elaborate stairway and in through two huge, wide-flung doors into a magnificent ballroom. The room was filled with people as bright and opulent as the mural-covered walls. I didn't know where to look next. Above me hung great chandeliers of shimmering glass. Around me swirled women in bright gowns and men in tight britches. I was completely agog with wonder.

Greg took things in his stride. He held my hand through the crook of his arm and led me into the crush of people. He obviously knew where he was going as he strode confidently forward. I was amazed by the way people parted around us, some stopping to say hello, others nodding their recognition. I smiled and trailed behind him, trying to walk elegantly in my gown and not trip over the hem.

Finally we reached our destination and Greg introduced me to the Conte and Contessa. They both wore blood red velvet and the Contessa's neck was decorated with several strings of sparkling necklaces. I felt instantly humbled, like a servant dressed in her mistress's best clothes. It was strange, I was used to meeting the rich and famous in my capacity as club manager, but these people of high standing in their ornate golden masks scared me stiff.

"So glad you could come, Greg, and with such a beautiful young lady on your arm."

I smiled and the conversation turned to business technicalities that I didn't understand. I turned to speak to the Contessa but she'd already moved on. She was clearly the person in charge because when she moved across the room, engaging in conversation with all the guests and giving directions to any members of staff she crossed paths with, she did it with such authority and confidence. She was clearly a formidable woman.

I was happy to watch the goings on around me. There was a jovial atmosphere behind the masks—I was sure most people could tell who they were talking to, but still, it added a little playfulness to the event. I wondered how many people would pluck up the courage to flirt with a person behind the safety curtain of their papier-mâché mask.

I plucked a glass from a tray that was offered to me and thanked the young girl before she waltzed off on her way. I admired her balance and poise, I was sure I'd have dropped a tray of champagne flutes if I'd attempted to carry them. Greg was still deep in conversation. I didn't mind too much, it was clearly a good opportunity for him to catch up with a serious business associate.

I watched those in the center of the room dancing to what even I with my lax knowledge of classical music knew was a Viennese Waltz. Maybe I'd watched an episode or two too many of *Strictly Come Dancing*. I wasn't sure it was totally time appropriate but the orchestral music, coming from a surprisingly small number of musicians huddled at one end of the hall, certainly sounded suitably classic for such a gathering.

"Sorry about that." Greg turned to me. "I thought it was best to get the business out of the way as soon as possible. Now I can focus on having a good time with you."

"Sounds fabulous to me," I replied with a huge grin. "This is amazing, isn't it?"

"Yeah." He pulled me into his body, and cupped his hand around my shoulder. "I've been to a few of the Conte's masquerades now but each time I'm taken by the scale and magnificence of it all."

We stood and watched for a while then Greg relieved me of my glass and dragged me to the center of the ballroom.

"I can't dance," I squealed. "Greg, I can't."

"Hush," he said. "Just follow my lead. It's a slow one, you'll be fine."

He clutched my waist and I laid a hand on his shoulder. The other hand he gripped tenderly in his hand and led me forward with a gentle tug.

I was going to protest, but as the music started I found myself too absorbed in not standing on anyone's toes to think about talking. It took a minute or so, but I did eventually get the hang of the steps.

"See" — he smirked — "I knew you'd get it."

I smiled at him. I was still not sure I could talk and dance at the same time, but I had to concede he was right. I enjoyed being swung around the floor, albeit elegantly, by his strong, demanding touch. I tingled with arousal as I followed his steps — our bodies barely touched but it felt like elaborate foreplay. He stared deep into my eyes when I finally lifted my head from looking at my feet and I could see the lust simmering in his expression behind his shiny, blue mask.

My dress moved magically around me, I didn't snag it once and the swishing made me feel lighthearted and free. I began to enjoy myself as I felt the music and didn't worry so much about the steps. When the song finished Greg and I stepped aside.

"When did you learn to dance?" I asked.

"Oh, early on. I had a girlfriend who was aristocracy. I needed to learn to dance to attend an event with her. She was a complete cow, but I will be forever thankful for the dancing lessons."

"You're very good," I whispered in his ear when he stopped to pick up a canapé from a silver tray held out by a butler. "I think you've got the hips for it."

"So have you," he returned, squeezing my waist with one hand and eating the caviar-decorated nibble in one bite.

"How long do we have to stay?" I asked. "I mean, it's fun but I'd prefer to dance with you naked, if you know what I mean."

"Oh, I know what you mean," he growled and pulled me into a full embrace. I flushed. I wasn't sure his rough behavior was suitable for such a setting. No one seemed to have noticed us, though. "But I think we can hang around here and have some fun still. Follow me."

"Really?"

"Oh, yeah, really." He leaned forward and kissed me. I wondered what kind of fun he meant. Surely sex was out of the question.

He pulled back after a long, slow kiss that curled my toes in their fine satin confines and pulled me behind him toward a table in the corner of the room that was laid out with edible delights. I looked at them and thought it would be great fun to eat but it wasn't quite what I needed to satisfy my appetite at that moment.

"Take a plate," Greg whispered in my ear, "and some food, then stand right here, by the wall."

I didn't know what he had planned but I followed his directions. One moment he was beside me then he wasn't. I picked a few items off the table and stood, plate in hand, at the very end of the trestle, back to the wall and side to the table. I picked at the food before me. I wasn't vastly hungry and even though the morsels were elegant and delicious I was too nervy to truly appreciate them.

What was Greg up to? As I watched the party twirling around me I realized one of the things I loved about Greg was that he kept me guessing. He was definitely not predictable.

I jumped when I felt my skirt being lifted at my side. I looked down and saw a blue shoulder between my dress and the white of the table. The pattern was very familiar and after a few seconds Greg was beneath my skirt.

I didn't know what to do. I tried to look nonchalant. I hoped no one had noticed what he'd done. I looked around me and conversations continued, the music played and dancers danced. It seemed that he'd pulled off the stealthy move.

Warm fingers curled around my ankle and I tried not to move. A strong hand traveled up my calf, onto my thigh and higher. I glanced around and smiled. I tried to give away nothing as Greg's touch rose between my thighs and he stroked over the crotch of my knickers.

I held fast, braced myself against the onslaught of arousal that coursed through me from his continued stroking. I didn't want to drop my plate, or knock the table or do anything else to draw attention. I remembered the food in my hand and decided I should at least try to eat something, just in case someone noticed.

I lifted a crisp piece of bread to my lips, smelling the creamy mozzarella and sharp tomato that sat on top of my bruschetta, along with the herbal hint of basil. I just had the tempting bite at lip level when Greg's questing finger found its way under the lace of my pretty underwear and into the warm cleft beneath. I moaned and hoped people would think it was at the delicious nature of the food.

I put the bread down again without taking a bite because he pressed on. His fingers sank into my giving flesh and I stretched around to accommodate him. His fingers repetitively sank into me and with each thrust I was certain my knees were going to give way under me and I'd collapse down onto him. I felt the fine satin of his jacket against my inner thigh and was aware of him shifting beneath me. His other arm wrapped over my hip and his other fingers dipped down into the groove of my pubis. His face was pressed against my buttocks, I could feel his breath moistening the back of my knickers and combined with the pressure on my clit and his fingers inside me I was as close to undone as a woman could be in so many clothes. I had to hold myself straight and try not to pant or moan out loud. I prayed no one would approach me. There was a crowd around, a queue of people along the buffet and many of them were within earshot. It was almost impossible to control the ecstasy that whizzed around my body as I built speedily to a climax.

I had to close my eyes when the orgasm overtook me. He bit my arse as I came and I bit hard down on my lip to stop from yelping. The pain of his teeth in my flesh carried the pleasure to the next level. I shook and shuddered and flicked open my eyes as soon as I could.

"Are you okay, miss?" a tall, thin old man in a black plague doctor mask asked.

"Oh, yes," I said. "Just a little warm, that's all."

The gentleman nodded. "You should get some fresh air, dear."

"I will," I replied, aware of Greg pulling his fingers from within me and replacing the crotch of my underwear to where it should be.

The kindly gentleman wandered off and I put my plate down on the table. I was sure I was going to drop it because I shook with the relief flowing through me.

"Enjoy that?" Greg appeared at my elbow and made me jump.

"Yes," I said with a nod, "and no. You're wicked."

"I am," he replied with a huge grin and a gloating laugh.

"I will have to plot my revenge," I continued. "But right now I need fresh air."

Greg led me over to a huge set of doors at the far end of the room but just when I felt the stirrings of a cooling breeze through the open door, the Conte stepped out and stopped Greg in his tracks.

"Greg, I've got someone I'd love you to meet." The Conte smiled brightly and Greg looked at me then back at the man before him.

"Sure, Conte." He smiled. "It would be a pleasure. Just one moment, please." He turned to me and continued in a bright, light tone. "Go outside for a breath of fresh air, I'll join you in a moment. Wait for me on the balcony, okay?"

"Sure." I smiled. "Don't be long. I'm starting to tire, I think I need to go to bed."

I gave him a playful smirk and he nodded. Greg walked back into the push of the crowd and I headed out of the impressive hall into the cool of the Venetian evening.

I was surprised by the length of the balcony when I reached the outside. It seemed to run the whole length of the building, with the one set of doors I'd walked out of and another farther along that could only go into a completely different room. There were a number of people on the balcony. A few couples cuddled together, oblivious to everything around them, and the odd single figure stared out over the canal below.

It was quiet and cool and I found a space along the railing to look out over the water myself. The cold air soothed my burning cheeks. I took in deep breaths. It had been a risky maneuver, but Greg was a man who did such things without thought. He wasn't the kind of person to let propriety dictate what he could or couldn't do.

I smiled. It might have scared the life out of me at the time, but it had also been one of the most intense orgasms of my life and it was certainly one I'd always remember. I was happy and I'd not even thought about work in nearly two days. I was mentally taking note to ring Taylor in the morning when I became aware of someone beside me.

I looked to the left and a man dressed all in black leaned there. He looked a bit like Zorro, which really didn't seem to fit in with the opulent, historical theme. I looked away again and a few seconds later I felt something hard poking at my side.

"Fancy meeting you here."

I froze. I knew that voice but surely it was too much of a coincidence.

"What? Cat got your tongue, Kerry? I know I have this stupid mask on but surely the ginger hair gives me away."

"Darren?"

"One and the same."

I looked to the side and yes, it was him. The bright hair, the cocky smirk.

"So, what are you doing here?" I started casually. I really wanted to run like billy-o to find Greg. If he saw me with his rival, God knew how he'd react.

"I'm here for you. Let's go."

"Darren, we've been over this." I sighed. "I'm not going anywhere with you. I'm here with Greg."

"Except he's in there and you're not. So that's not technically true. Also, I've got a gun pressed to the bottom of your ribs. I really don't want to hurt you but I do want to talk to you, alone. So, I suggest you turn slowly and walk toward the exit over there."

My heart stopped, or so it felt, then leaped up into my throat. I couldn't think, I couldn't breathe. Suddenly my floaty frock was a prison and it constricted my chest painfully. All I could feel was that weight at my hip. All I could think of was that I was seconds away from being dead.

I had no choice, I honestly couldn't think of anything to do but to walk slowly toward the other door.

"Good girl," he growled, and I prayed that Greg would walk out and see. I prayed that something heavy would fall from the sky directly on his head. Anything at all to stop me in my tracks. Sadly, nothing happened. We negotiated our way through the house down to the canal. Of course, there was a water taxi waiting and no one, not a single person pointed out that I was leaving with a different man than I had arrived with.

"What are you doing, Darren?" I asked when finally the taxi pulled away.

"I'm enjoying a little break in Venice, Kerry, what about you?"

"Well, apparently I'm being kidnapped by a big kid who can't take it when a woman tells him no."

"Who also has a fucking gun aimed at you, Kerry. You might want to take that into account before you throw insults about." Darren waved said gun around and I shut up because I had no idea if there were bullets in it or not but I didn't want to take the chance.

My mind whirred. I didn't have a phone on me — I was in an old-style dress and had had nowhere to put it. I certainly didn't have any pigeons on me to send with a message and although I knew how to do an SOS in semaphore I had nothing to dot dot dash dash with. I was stuck.

"So, I saw you and Greg in the newspaper this morning, here in Venice, enjoying yourselves and looking all in love. Up to that moment I'd almost forgotten about you, how you broke my heart."

I couldn't believe what I was hearing. I'd shagged him a time or two, yes, but there had never been the emotional connection between Darren and I that I enjoyed with Greg. How could he say I'd broken his heart?

"But I saw you and I knew I had to have you. So I jumped on my jet and kept checking my Twitter. I saw you get your designer frock and your hand-crafted mask and I knew you'd be going to one place tonight, and I was right."

"Look, Darren, I don't want to upset you, but why? Why've you done all this?" It was a long shot, but I wondered if maybe I could talk some sense into him.

"Why not? I tried my best to win you back, Kerry. I sent you so many gifts, I tried to show you just how much I cared, but you ignored it and you ended up with him. You chose that dull prat Greg over me. Clearly I needed to do something to prove to you that I love you more than he does."

Darren sat beside me, uncomfortably close. I didn't look at him, I kept looking straight ahead. I could see buildings, their shadows and the lit windows as they passed and I could hear the roar of the engine and the gargle of the water. I had no idea where we were going and had no way to escape.

"Look at me, Kerry," he demanded. I turned my head. "I'm here to claim what is rightfully mine. I'm here to claim you."

He pushed his face up against mine and kissed me. I kept stone still. I didn't move forward or back but I did not return the kiss and he growled in frustration after he pulled away.

"What the fuck is wrong with you?"

"What's wrong?" I could feel the anger bubbling up inside me over the fear. "What's wrong? Where the fuck do I start?"

"Language." He pushed the gun into my side again and I sighed. I really wanted to give him a damn good tongue-lashing, but I couldn't. I was at his mercy and that scared me to death. I swallowed down my anger and answered plainly and as dispassionately as I could.

"I don't love you, Darren. I'm sorry, but that's the truth."

"How do you know?" he replied, his Scouse accent getting thicker with every sentence he uttered. "How can you say that when you've not even given me a decent chance?"

"Look, Darren, I know it's difficult for you to see me with Greg and all but—"

"You can say that again," he exclaimed. "That greasy bastard is no good for you, Kerry, trust me. He was my best mate once, did you know that, eh? Did yer?"

"No." I shook my head. "I didn't." I hoped that if I kept him talking he'd drop his guard and I could grab his gun. Then the tables would be turned and maybe I could escape and make things all right again.

"Well, we were. We went to uni together. I helped Greg produce his first bit of useful code. A game. We were supposed to split the proceeds fifty-fifty but the bastard shafted me on it. Not only did he steal my game and my royalties, he was sleeping with my girlfriend at the time too, the girlfriend he knew I was going to propose to. So you know when I found out? On the day I was going to propose. He was making out with her on the beach where I'd arranged to meet Paula. I had the ring in my pocket and everything and Greg stood there and kissed her. He never even apologized. He just shrugged."

How did I answer that? I didn't, I kept quiet.

"So, you see, I'm doing you a favor. He didn't stick with her, no, he threw her to the side once he'd ruined things for me. Can you see what he's capable of? He's only going to break your heart."

"People change," I replied succinctly.

"He hasn't changed, Kerry, he's just a charming git. He'll be nice as pie while he wants something from you, then when he's got it, he'll leave you high and dry."

"Well, thanks for the info, Darren, but I'm an adult. I can make my own decisions."

"Clearly not," he snapped back. "How could you pick him over me?"

"So it does come down to that, then. I picked him over you and you can't stand it."

"Yes, yes, it does. He's a prick, Kerry."

"Well, you've kidnapped me at gunpoint, Darren, what am I supposed to make of that?"

Just then the boat engine silenced and the taxi pulled up to a stop. Darren dug the gun into my side.

"Move it," he growled.

I wondered if Greg had discovered I was missing as I stepped off the boat and walked just ahead of Darren who pressed his hand into the bottom of my back and his gun into my hip. I wondered what he'd be doing. Would he be looking for me? I had to hope so. I couldn't see any way to save myself.

Darren led me to a house, nothing special, and he unlocked the door. I wondered about making a run for it, but it was too risky. My elegant skirts would hamper me and I was sure they'd be little protection from a speeding bullet.

Chapter Nine

I was a little surprised when Darren locked me in the upper room in the not-so-grand house and left me there. I did a thorough sweep of the area but found no way to escape or anything to use as a weapon. All that sat in the threadbare prison was a bed, just a simple divan, so no spindles to break or metal poles to unscrew. It didn't even have a pillow or a duvet.

I sat on it once I'd worn myself out trying to open the window, a stupid plastic double-glazed affair that was disgustingly well fitted. I tried the door too, but it was thick and locked with several bolts, which I'd heard when he left and clicked them all shut.

You never expect to be kidnapped, I'm sure, but I certainly hadn't been expecting my perfect, fairy tale trip to turn into a crime thriller. I was petrified but I knew that panicking and getting het up wouldn't help me. I wanted to scream and shout and bawl — I did for a little while — but with the double glazing, thick doors and walls I was sure no one would hear me.

I didn't know what Darren would do with me. I didn't think he would be capable of killing me, but then he was the one with the gun and the plan. Would he hold me here against my will forever? Would he rape me? I'd taken a self-defense course when I first established Diamonds and I was pretty sure I could inflict some pain on him if I got the opportunity to do so, but if I did escape would I live forever in fear of him?

I had no way to record what was happening to me. The only people who'd seen us on the way out of the party had probably thought we were an average couple. There hadn't been any hint that I was being forced from the party. The only person who might have seen anything was the guy who had picked us up in the water taxi, but I was sure he'd have been concentrating on steering and not looking over his shoulder to see what was happening in his boat.

I had lost all track of time. It was still dark out when Darren returned so I knew he'd not been gone for more than a few hours.

"Sorry about that." He smiled menacingly when he came into the room. He locked the door behind him. It was just one key, one lock from the inside I noted, Maybe that would be my way out. "Business called, you know how it is."

I didn't answer. I didn't even look up at him.

"So, where were we?" He came over and sat on the bed beside me.

My heart raced, my mouth felt dry and I felt a sudden stab of cold on the bottom of my back that seeped up through me to saturate my limbs. I shivered.

"Oh, are you cold?" Darren put his arm around me and I didn't feel any warmer. I wanted to pull away but I could see that damn gun in his lap, gray and menacing.

"Darren," I gasped, "what are you doing? I don't understand."

"I'm making you change your mind," he said.

"Look, I can't talk to you with that gun pointed at me. Take it away, please? Lock it away somewhere. What harm can I do you? You've got the upper hand even without the weapon."

He looked at me, then down at the gun he cradled.

"Right, fine. I'll be back in a minute." He stood up, walked over to the door and let himself out. I let out a heavy sigh of breath. It wasn't much more of a chance, but without the gun, I could talk to him and at least know I wasn't going to end up instantly dead. I still wasn't sure I could overpower him. Though I'd done that self-defense class years ago, I wasn't a kung fu master by any stretch of the imagination.

When Darren returned he once again sat on the bed with me. "Right, go ahead. Talk." He turned to me.

"Okay." I worried my fingers together in my lap as I searched for what to say. He might not have a weapon pointed at me, but he was still an impulsive man well capable of striking out if he heard something he didn't like. "I just want to know something first—do you really think this is a good way to persuade me I picked the wrong guy?"

"Well, clearly this is not the avenue I'd have chosen if you weren't so damn stubborn. You wouldn't answer my calls or emails and you've not been in your club for days. I was waiting there for you, I wanted to talk to you. I needed to get you alone. That is what I've now done."

"But, Darren, you've violated any trust I had in you. You brought me here against my will. You could have talked to me at the Conte's party."

"Where he could walk in at any minute? I think not." Darren scowled. It made him look truly ugly. I saw years of bitterness etched on his creased brow. "No, I needed to get you away from him."

"If you had asked, I'd have arranged to meet you another time. I'm not heartless, you know. We could have arranged to meet up once I got home. We could have talked it all out like the grown-ups we're meant to be."

"Bullshit," he hissed, the sibilance of his accent running through the last syllable and spattering spittle in its intensity. "You'd just go back to ignoring me. I couldn't risk that, I couldn't leave you with him, knowing what he could do to you."

"Greg would never hurt me," I responded flatly, not wanting to raise my voice and upset my captor. "I know you don't like him, but really and truthfully, is this about your concern about my well-being or is it more about you being jealous?"

Darren sat silently for a moment. The bitterness was clearly evident in his relaxed features. Maybe I hadn't noticed them before, but now I could see the dark marks of jealousy and hate evident in the way he held his jaw and ensconced deep within him. I saw it in his eyes.

"I can't deny that I'm envious of him. I can't deny that I'm pissed off that you picked him over me, but that isn't all of it. He is a seriously twisted man, Kerry."

"Can't you see the irony in that?" I laughed with hysteria. "You're the one who kidnapped me."

"Don't laugh," he whispered and shot his hand out to grip my upper arm painfully tight.

"Sorry." I took a breath and stopped myself.

"I haven't kidnapped you," he continued. "You are free to leave whenever you like."

"Then I'd like—"

"No, no, you have to hear me out first. You've not even tried to see it from my point of view, Kerry. I'm seriously disappointed in you. I thought you were different, I thought you were someone special. I thought we could have a future together. That's why I agreed to share you that night, because I wanted to get closer to you and I was willing to do anything to get you."

His words were chilling, though they sounded like they'd come straight from a romantic novel. The emotion behind them wasn't love, it was obsession. I kept silent.

"I was so good to you, Kerry. I treated you like a queen. I'd give you anything, absolutely anything you want. All you need to do is choose me. Forget him, resist his smarmy lure and you'll be happy. I'll make you happy, Kerry."

I shook my head.

"Darren, I make my own happiness. I don't need a man to make me happy. I don't need a man to buy me things, I don't need a man to be whole. I am the one who dictates my happiness. I make my decisions and I won't take bribes and I won't be forced to make a decision I don't want. This is coercion, Darren. This is madness. I don't want you, get it?"

Sadness ripped across his face and mingled with the bitterness etched there. I didn't know what he was capable of, so I thought before I said anything more.

"Look, I know it's difficult. I shouldn't have led you both on in the first place. I was greedy. I was in the wrong. However, I made my decision, Darren, and I stand by it."

"Maybe this will change your mind." Darren kissed me.

He pushed me back and I fell across the bed beneath him. I couldn't return the kiss, I couldn't stand the weight of him above me, but a crazed idea zoomed into my mind and instinct made me go with it. As Darren settled above me, his thighs split around me. I scrambled back. He followed and we twisted and turned until we were in the center of the bed, head to the wall.

He continued to kiss me. I lifted my hands and gripped his hips. Then with all my might I lifted my knee and struck him directly in the nuts and at the same moment I braced my arms and forced his body forward until I heard the crunch of his head hitting the wall.

I was a little surprised when he slumped onto me. I'd been expecting a fight, maybe to have to hit his head a couple of times more. Maybe I didn't know my own strength.

I had to use it all to flip him off me. I stuck my hand into his pocket and pulled out his keys. I paused for a moment and checked he was breathing with my hand over his mouth. He was. I rolled him onto his side, not quite in the recovery position but it would keep him from swallowing his own tongue while he was out cold.

Yeah, he was a bastard but I didn't want to kill him. I scrambled through the keys, hands trembling, and found the one that fitted in the lock. I turned it, opened the door and ran, as well as I could in my dress. I ran down the stairs and into the street.

Chapter Ten

The light hint of dawn was pinkening the sky and I just ran up the street away from the house. I kept running. The streets were nigh on deserted. No one stopped me or asked me what I was doing.

I ran until I couldn't do it anymore. I stood with my back to a wall and drank in gulps of air. I had to work out where I was so I could get back to the hotel. I looked around – there was a café across the road and a young lady was setting chairs out around the tables outside.

"Excuse me," I said when I approached, "do you speak English?"

"Little." She smiled.

"I need to get to the Ca Dei Contei hotel, which way?"

She looked puzzled.

"Ca Dei Contei?" I replied, hoping I had the pronunciation somewhat right.

"That way." She pointed to her left. "To canal. Ask canal."

I was sure she didn't expect me to get directions from the water itself, but it made sense. If I could find a water taxi, they'd be able to give me directions.

"*Grazie*," I replied and walked at a more sedate pace in the direction she'd pointed. It wasn't far to the canal, unsurprisingly I supposed. There didn't seem to be many people there, however, so I looked up and down for concentrations of boats and headed toward a clump of them farther along the waters. On my way I met a man walking a little dog. It was a mixture of goodness only knows what, small and squat and scruffy.

"Excuse me," I said, "do you speak English?"

"Yes," he replied confidently. He smiled broadly, his wrinkly face wiggling with the movement.

"Do you know the way to the Ca Dei Contei hotel?"

He nodded slowly, his chins expanding and compressing when he did so.

"It is best by water," he said.

"Oh, I have no money." I shrugged. "I need to walk."

He looked me up and down. I was sure I looked a state and felt my first pang of regret at how dirty and abused Stephano's beautiful gown had become.

"Follow me." He beckoned. "Mitzi and I will show you."

"Thank you so much," I sighed. I suppose I shouldn't have trusted him, even though his soft face told of many years of kindness, but I was just too tired to think and I certainly didn't want to doubt my rescuer.

He walked me down to a busy interchange on the waterfront and headed toward the jetty.

"But I have no—"

He stopped my words with a shake of his hand then approached a driver and pressed some notes into the captain's grasp.

"Go with my friend Giuseppe, he will take you to your hotel."

My eyes welled up with tears. I was so touched by the kindness of this stranger. "Thank you so much." I gasped and he just smiled broadly.

"You're welcome, *signora*, it is my pleasure to help."

"Thank you," I repeated myself as I scurried onto the floating taxi. "Thank you," I shouted again before ducking into the cabin. The kind old man just smiled and waved.

I wept then. The kindness of a stranger had opened the well of deep emotion within me. I let all my emotions roll out of me for just a few moments then I steadied myself. I was away from him now, I was nearly back to Greg, it was going to be okay.

I stepped into the hotel and confidently strode toward the reception desk. "Excuse me, do you know if Greg Stamford is in his room?" I didn't want to go all the way up there if he wasn't—I didn't have a key and I wanted to see Greg as soon as possible.

"Oh, no." The slim, immaculately suited young lady behind the desk shook her head. "He checked out last night."

"Last night?" I gasped. "No, that can't be right. We're here together."

She nodded. "There is a note, *signora*. Your things are in left luggage. Would you like me to get them for you?"

I nodded mutely, not sure what was happening to me. Why had Greg left? Wasn't he worried about me? He'd stranded me in a foreign country, it didn't seem right.

The young girl came back a moment later with my suitcase.

"Just a moment, there is the letter here for you too." She stepped back behind her desk and passed me an envelope. I took it from her and pulled my luggage back where I'd come from. My purse was at the top of my case. I pulled it out and checked its contents. I had a little cash and my credit card so I hoped they'd be enough to get me back home. I tried to push down my emotional response and thought only of the practical. I went to wait for a water taxi to take me to the airport.

"Will you take English money?" I asked. I'd not had time to change any to euros, Greg had paid for everything. The captain nodded and I climbed aboard his boat.

The long walk from the water taxi port to the main airport was torturous. People stared at me in my tattered finery. I hadn't opened the letter, I was scared to find out its contents. When I reached the airport I went to find the next flight back to London. I had a wait of four hours. When I'd paid for my ticket I took myself and my luggage to the ladies.

I peeled myself from my ball gown and pulled jeans and a T-shirt from my bag. It was difficult undressing and dressing in a cubicle but once I was in my civilian clothes I felt better. I put the gown into my bag with as much care as I could manage and after lowering the toilet lid I sat down and opened the note.

I can't believe you left the party with him. Did you plan this all along?

I was falling in love with you... How could you be so cruel?

Don't try to answer that. I'm going home. I hope you and Darren will be very happy together. You make a good couple, you're both two-faced.

I didn't just cry, I sobbed. I sobbed long and hard until my shoulders shook and my throat seized up with dryness.

"Excuse me, miss, are you all right?" A voice from outside the cubicle echoed around the tiled room.

"Yes." I sniffed. "Yes, I'll be all right."

I blew my nose and pulled myself out of the loos. I smiled apologetically to the cleaner wiping around the sinks whose voice I'd earlier heard.

"Sorry about that," I apologized.

"It's okay," she replied with a concerned smile. "Take care, okay?"

It made me chuckle dispassionately that the only kindness I'd been shown all day had come from total strangers. I took myself to a coffee shop, ordered a large cup of dark coffee and a bottle of water. I knocked back the water to alleviate my thirst then sipped the hot drink for comfort.

I took my phone from my pocket. It still had a very small amount of charge. I clicked on Greg's number and held the phone to my ear. It went straight to voicemail.

"Greg, I need to tell you what really happened. I'm so sorry and I was so scared." My voice caught and a tear rolled down my cheek. "I didn't go with Darren of my own accord, Greg, he made me leave the Conte's with him. Please believe me, please?" I couldn't say anything else, I was crying and shaking again. I clicked end and slipped the mobile back into my pocket.

I picked up a napkin and wiped my eyes. I'd told Darren I didn't need anyone, I'd told him I was independent. Well, it was time that I proved it to myself. Who was there for me to go to for help? No one. I'd have to get over it myself. I wondered if Darren was awake yet, if I'd done any permanent damage in the wake of my escape. I hoped he wasn't on my tail. What would he do if he found me at the airport?

He didn't find me at the airport, he wasn't on the flight or waiting on my doorstep. Neither was Greg. When I got in, early in the evening, I rang Taylor at the club.

"Oh, so you're back then," he said when he heard it was me. "I thought you'd fallen off the end of the earth."

"Sorry about that, I was a little distracted. Is everything okay there?"

"Fine and dandy, boss. It's running like clockwork."

"Wonderful. I'll be back in tomorrow, okay? Right now, I need to sleep."

"Okay, no worries. Are you all right, boss? You don't sound like yourself."

"No, yeah, I'm fine." I rubbed my temples. "Just tired. I'll see you tomorrow, okay?"

"Sure," he replied. "See ya."

I crawled into bed. I'd not eaten or slept in close to twenty-four hours. I wasn't hungry but I was tired. I curled up and willed myself to switch off. I dozed a little but I kept waking, startled by noises real or imagined. I checked my phone—its battery was dead so I plugged it in. I went to sit in the front room and put the TV on for company. It was ten o'clock and the news was on.

"Billionaire Darren Bennett was treated in hospital for a head wound and suspected concussion after being attacked by masked robbers. The mobile media mogul was rushed into Venice hospital early this morning and his doctor has described his condition as comfortable. It is thought that Mr Bennett had been in Venice for Carnival and was attacked on his way home from a party."

I was relieved to hear that he was alive and also that I wasn't Britain's Most Wanted. Would he report me, though? Who would the police believe in that situation? I had no proof that he had kidnapped me but I supposed my DNA would be all over him. I had to hope that Darren didn't want to admit to being knocked out by a girl.

I fell asleep on the sofa, the TV humming in the background. I was completely worn down. When I woke the phone was ringing.

"Hello?" I answered, hoping to God that it was Greg.

"Hello, boss." Taylor's familiar tone was not the voice I wanted to hear.

"Oh, hey."

"Have you got a minute? The beer delivery hasn't turned up and when I rang the brewery they were less than helpful."

"Sure," I replied. "I'll give them a ring then I'll make my way in."

"Brill, thanks, boss."

I slipped into the shower and washed away the grime and attempted to scrub away the sadness. I dressed myself and became Kerry Matthews again. I was the boss of a successful club and restaurant and I had to concentrate on that. My business was all that mattered.

Chapter Eleven

It was a long and hard day at work, just what I needed. I threw myself into it, concentrating solely on what I was doing, not allowing my thoughts to drift.

"Hey, did you hear that Darren bloke was attacked?" Taylor commented as he leaned casually against the bar.

"Yeah, saw it on the news. Is he out of hospital yet?"

"I dunno. Funny thing was, he was in Venice at the time."

"Was he?" I replied, cagily.

"Funny that, you and Greg were there too, right?"

"Yeah." I nodded. "We didn't see him, though. Lots of rich people go to Venice for Carnival."

"True." He nodded. "How is Greg?"

"Okay, I guess." I shrugged.

"Oh, don't tell me you've fallen out again."

"Look, Taylor, I don't want to talk about it." I shook my head.

"All right, boss. I'll shut up. But you know I'm here if you need me, right?"

I nodded and smiled through the stupid tears that had bubbled up unbidden. "Thanks," I replied.

"Just because you're a strong, independent woman, Kerry, doesn't mean you have to deal with everything on your own." He reached over the bar and squeezed my arm.

"Thanks," I said again. "I'll be okay."

It was when I lay in bed checking my phone for the millionth time at three a.m. that I realized I wasn't going to be okay. As much as I tried to ignore it, to carry on regardless, to be angry with Greg for abandoning me, I just felt sad. I needed to see him, to explain what had gone wrong.

The problem was I didn't know his address. In all our time together we'd met at mine or in exotic locations, I'd never been to his home. I had his phone number, but he wasn't answering the phone and he'd not replied to my text asking him to ring me. I had no other way of contacting him.

I lay awake thinking it over for a while, and my phone rang. I picked it up, convinced it would be Greg.

"You bitch." A familiar, cold voice greeted me.

"Darren?"

"Yes," he growled. "You didn't kill me."

"I didn't want to," I protested. "I just wanted to get away from my kidnapper—you."

"Well, news for you, you didn't get away. You just made things worse for yourself."

"Why, what do you mean?" I sat bolt upright and nibbled on my bottom lip.

"I was offering you the world, Kerry, I was offering you my hand in marriage but now, I'm going to put all my energies into destroying you."

"What?" I gasped. "Don't be silly, Darren."

"Silly? I'm not being silly, you fucking knocked me out, you bitch. You rejected me for him."

I laughed bitterly. "Oh, you'll get a kick out of this," I sighed. "Greg abandoned me. He just left the hotel and let me make my own way home. He thought I'd left the party with you purposefully."

"Really?" Darren cackled. It was the scariest sound I'd ever heard. "Ha, well, isn't that just peachy?" He laughed some more. "The icing on the cake, then, I don't have to break you guys up, saves me a job. I just have to destroy your business. That saves me some time."

"Pardon?"

"You heard me. Diamonds. I'm going to break it down and then I'm going to buy it and I'm going to kick you out on the streets."

"Well, good luck with that," I replied. "Diamonds is mine. I'm not going to give up without a fight."

"That's what I was hoping," he sneered and put down the phone on me.

I was frantic. What was he going to do? I wouldn't let him take the club from me, I *couldn't* let him take it from me. But how was I going to protect it?

The next day it became clear what Darren's first move was going to be. "Are you sure you want to cancel?" I said to the third person that day. "I can assure you that— Oh, okay, well, that is of course your decision. If you'd like to rebook for another date..."

I slammed the phone down.

"Another one?"

I nodded.

"That bastard." I'd told Taylor that Darren had a bee in his bonnet. I'd not told him more than that, but he needed to have an idea of what was going on. "We'll be all right, though, boss. He's not friends with every person in London, you'll still get plenty of business."

"Hmm, you might want to read this."

Shelly put an open newspaper down on the table in front of us. It was a review of Diamonds and it wasn't pleasant.

"This is all lies," Taylor snapped. "I've never served dodgy beer in my life and the chef is top notch."

I shook my head. That was just the start of my problems. When the chef got wind of the bad review, he left in a huff. We had an unannounced visit from Environmental Health, which, of course, gave us the all-clear but we were told that serious allegations had been brought so we'd be under continual observation. By the time the bar had shut that night I was ready to pull all my hair out I was so stressed.

It didn't get any easier, either. The only thing that kept me going was the customers. There was one afternoon when the beer delivery hadn't turned up and the freezer had mysteriously been turned down too low and we'd had a brick through a window the night before and the glazier still hadn't turned up. I still had on my plastered fake smile and I was out waiting on tables as Jen had given birth to a little girl and was off on maternity leave.

"Oh, Kerry, we had to come," an old man exclaimed when I went to take their order. "We saw that terrible review in the paper and we had to come. We couldn't believe it was true, could we, dear?"

The white, curly-haired old lady opposite nodded.

"Well, you're very kind." I smiled. "I hope you do find your experience here today pleasurable."

"I'm sure we will," Harry continued. "I love Diamonds. I might be a bit long in the tooth now but I still feel welcome here and so does my darling wife, Dorothy, don't you, dear?"

Dorothy nodded and smiled again.

"I am glad," I replied. "Now can I get you something to drink or to eat?"

They gave me their order and I couldn't help but smile a real, genuine smile as I served them. Such a sweet couple, and even though they weren't quite in the demographic of most of Diamonds' customers, they still felt at home. That made me feel warm deep inside and at the time it was colder than the Antarctic in there.

"Kerry," Harry said to me when I processed his credit card to pay his bill. "I'm very happy to say that the review we read was complete poppycock. We've had a lovely time, you've been so good to us and the food was delicious."

"Well, thank you," I replied, feeling a little choked at his kind words.

"You've got nothing to worry about, dear. I'll be telling everyone how good Diamonds is and Dorothy will too, won't you, dear?"

Dorothy nodded and I smiled.

It was Harry and Dorothy and the other customers who continued to come and fill my bar and my restaurant who kept me going. So much went wrong but our numbers didn't waver. We lost a few big events, but the general public still loved Diamonds. We never seemed any quieter and my books still balanced perfectly well. Darren was not doing a great job of running my bar into the ground—the bar's owner was on the brink of a nervous breakdown, though.

I was in work every day, not purposefully, but every time I tried to get some time off, something went wrong. I was completely worn out and I wondered if that was Darren's plan, simply to grind me down until I gave him the damn place.

In four weeks I dealt with every emergency you could imagine, and some you wouldn't believe. I supposed the only advantage to it was that I didn't have time to think about anything else, like Greg. Thoughts of him crept in fairly regularly and my sleep was filled with dreams featuring him, some good, some raging nightmares. As much as I wanted to forget him completely, it just wasn't happening.

The worst day of my life was a Tuesday. I got up, got dressed and got the Tube. I was ready for whatever the day was going to throw at me. I wasn't feeling good but I felt prepared to do whatever I had to do.

I was *not* prepared to see my beautiful club enrobed in smoke and flames. Three fire engines were outside, hoses aimed at the center of the blaze. I pushed through the crowd of onlookers to a streak of plastic tape that seemed to hold them back. I went to dip under it but I was stopped in my tracks by a policeman who seemed to be as wide as he was tall.

"Sorry, miss, you can't come through here, it's too dangerous."

"But it's my club," I gasped, tears flowing down my cheeks. "It's my life."

"You're the owner then?" I nodded.

And so started a morning of answering asinine questions and fending off horrific accusations at the local police station.

"I don't know," I said. "For the last time, I have no idea what might have caused it."

Eventually I was released, with a strict instruction to not leave the country. I wanted to go back to the club, but I wasn't allowed to. If I got too close I might try to fuck up the evidence. I rang Taylor instead.

"I dunno, boss. Everything seemed fine when we left, I can't believe what's happened."

"No, neither can I." I sighed. "Will you ring round the staff? Tell them I'll pay them their usual shifts but I don't know when we'll get the club back open—if people want to seek employment elsewhere, I won't hold it against them."

"Okay, boss, I'll get on it. Jeez, this sucks."

"Yeah, it does."

I knew exactly who was to blame for the fire—Darren had to be behind it somewhere along the line. I doubted he'd have personally set the place alight but he would have been involved. How it could be proven, I didn't know, but I'd have to try. I couldn't come to terms with what I'd seen—all my hard work, all my dreams up in smoke.

It would take months to repair and God knew how much longer to get the insurance paid out. I'd have to start from scratch again. I couldn't face going home and looking at the four walls there so I just walked. I didn't know what to do. I wanted someone to talk to, someone to hold me and tell me it'd be all right and my traitorous mind went to one person only—Greg. I wanted Greg.

I admit I was probably not thinking very rationally. I certainly wasn't making any sense, not even to myself, but I had to find Greg.

I started out by discovering where he worked. That is the gift of smartphones—you can stalk anyone on the go without having to find an A–Z or a phone book. It was a short Tube journey over to the center of the financial district and when I emerged onto the street I was faced by dozens of people in smart suits carrying briefcases and over-the-shoulder laptop bags.

I'd never really seen the attraction of office work. I'd always been a social character and always had my eye on a job that involved some kind of interaction with people. I was made to be in customer services, it was my perfect job.

It didn't take long to find the office block that housed Greg's place of work. The whole tower was dedicated to different branches of his empire—the mobile phone apps, the mobile phone network, the computer game brand he owned, they all had their headquarters there. It was a tall, glass-fronted structure, minimalist and efficient-looking. If I'd been more myself I would have thought twice about walking up to the huge front doors and striding across the marble floor to the sleek, wood-fronted reception desk.

While I waited for the thin, immaculately attired receptionist to finish on the phone I glanced at the board beside her. Unsurprisingly, Greg's office was on the very top floor. It would have an amazing view over the city, I was sure. After a minute the lady rested the phone receiver in its cradle once more and looked up at me.

"Can I help you?" she asked.

"I'd like to see Greg Stamford, please."

"Certainly, miss." The lady at the desk beamed. "Do you have an appointment?"

"Erm, no," I replied.

"Ah." She sucked air in through her teeth. "Mr Stamford is rather busy this afternoon, you're best making an appointment to see him."

"When is he next available?"

"I believe we have a slot at the end of next week, I had someone cancel this morning."

"Oh, well, I really need to see him today," I replied steadily, even though I was starting to feel panicky inside.

"Well, I can show you to the waiting room, miss, then I can find out if he has time to fit you in. What's your name?"

"That would be great, thank you. My name is Kerry Matthews."

The lady's eyes widened and her perfectly painted bottom lip dropped for a fraction of a second before she raised it again. She had regained her composure within a matter of moments.

"Ah, well, I have been informed that Mr Stamford doesn't want to see you at all, I'm afraid."

"Look, this is really important, I wouldn't be here otherwise."

"I understand that." She bobbed her head and her short blonde hair bobbed up and down slickly in line. "But it would be more than my job's worth to even ask him to see you, miss. Mr Stamford was very forceful about the matter."

I felt a tear slip down my cheek as all bravado and false confidence melted away with her words.

"Look." She smiled sympathetically. "Let me show you into the waiting room. You can sit and compose yourself for a while, all right? I'm sorry I can't do anything more."

I nodded and followed her down the corridor into a room that housed a large coffee table and half a dozen or so comfy-looking gray chairs.

"I'll come back and check on you in a little while," she said. "Take all the time you need."

I nodded and sat down. I'd come so far, I wasn't ready to give up. I looked around the room and wondered how I could get to Greg's office.

I walked over to the door she'd led me in by, the only one in the room. To the left was her desk, to the right, more corridor. I waited until there was someone at the receptionist's desk blocking her view down the corridor, then I carefully swung open the door, thankful it didn't have squeaky hinges, and took off down the hall away from the entrance, trying hard to make sure my work shoes didn't squeak on the shiny wood floor. I soon found an access point to the staircase and ducked in through the double doors. I imagined most people would use the lift and I would have preferred to myself, knowing how many floors high the building was. But it was back in the foyer, past the reception and the security guards, so it was simply not an option.

I hurried up the first three flights, convinced someone would come running after me at any moment. I had to slow down then, though, because although I wasn't exactly unfit with the work I did at Diamonds, I wasn't exactly an athlete either. I didn't have the stamina to keep running, especially not up steps.

As I suspected, no one used the stairs. They were simply there in case of emergencies. When I made it to the seventh and eighth floors without detection, I started to calm down a bit. I kept climbing. I knew it would take time—this was not a short building and although I was losing count of the flights I'd walked up, I was sure that I was probably only halfway to Greg's office. My legs throbbed by the time I reached floor seventeen. I stood to one side of the doorway for a few minutes to capture my breath. I still had a few flights to climb and I wanted to be capable of speech once I got there.

As I stood, hands on knees, back bent and panting like a fluffy dog in the middle of summer, the door beside me swung open. I held my breath. The door hid me for a moment and the woman ran up the stairs in the other direction. As her heels clattered I let out a sigh of relief. Once I was capable of breathing and not panting I continued up the stairs at a sedate pace — that way if I was passed by the woman coming back down, I hoped she'd mistake me for a fellow worker. That wouldn't happen if I was bright red in the face, sweating and huffing and puffing like I'd just run the marathon.

Finally I reached the top floor. I stopped again and peered through the small glass windows of the door. There was another receptionist's desk then a door that I assumed led into Greg's office. On closer inspection I saw his name on the plaque on the door, confirming my suspicion. The desk was empty when I looked and so, before I had time to think and talk myself out of it, I strode through the door, past the desk and into Greg's office without pausing to knock.

The room was huge — every wall was in fact windows, apart from the one housing the door I'd just walked through. Greg's desk was directly opposite me and he sat behind it in a tall-backed leather chair. A small woman sat on a far more square and practical chair with her back to me.

I couldn't speak, all words clogged up in my throat. I just wanted to run over to him and fling my arms around his neck but I couldn't even propel myself forward anymore. Greg looked up and his expression barely changed. He lifted his eyebrows briefly then looked back down to the woman opposite him.

"That's it for today, Samantha," he said. "You can go home now."

"If you're sure," she said, darting a look from the paper pad in her hand to the door and me as she made to stand.

"I am." He nodded. "Just let Barney know I have a visitor when you leave, please."

"Certainly, sir. See you tomorrow."

The young girl stood and sashayed across the floor. Her outfit was highly practical and smart at first look, then you noticed the low V of her blouse that showed off ample cleavage, the three-inch heels on her black shoes and the tight cut of her jacket. She scowled when she walked past me and I couldn't have cared less.

When the door clicked shut Greg was the first to speak.

"How did you get in?"

"The stairs," I replied, still glued to the spot beside the door.

"Really? That's a long way up."

"Yeah." I nodded. "A really long way."

"Jeez, Kerry, what do I have to do to keep you away from me?"

I shrugged. "I should apologize to the receptionist. She was very nice to me. I shed a few tears and she let me compose myself in the waiting room. I then completely broke her trust by sneaking off. Don't punish her for it, please? She was very good at her job."

"Not good enough to keep you out, though." Greg sighed and ran a hand through his dark hair. "Well, now you're here you'd better come and sit down. I don't suppose you'll go if I ask you to, will you?"

"Just let me say my piece then if you still want me to leave, I'll leave."

Greg nodded curtly. He knotted his fingers together and rested them in his lap.

I forced myself to move forward and sat down in the chair opposite him. I wanted to reach out and touch him, I wanted to lean over the desk and kiss him, but I knew that those actions would lead to trouble so I reined myself in.

"Okay, so I guess I should start where we left off, in Venice." I sighed deeply. My heart palpitated, and not just from the exertion I'd put myself through. "I didn't leave that masquerade of my own accord, Greg. I was waiting on the balcony, cooling down and thinking about you when Darren arrived. I didn't know he'd be there, I didn't want him to be there but he appeared beside me and oh, God, I know this sounds far-fetched, but he held a gun to my side and made me leave with him."

Greg didn't show any sign of reaction to what I told him. He was stony-faced, his body held stiffly in his chair, his hands tightly entwined before him.

"I was completely petrified the whole time but as long as he had the gun I couldn't do anything. I wanted to scream, I wanted to run away but I couldn't because I was afraid he'd shoot me. He was completely psychotic. Kept telling me it was all for my own good, that I'd picked the wrong man and he was trying to protect me from you. He really didn't see that he was doing anything wrong, it was creepy."

Greg was still impassive. I carried on.

"He took me to some house and locked me in a room. All it had was a bed. I had no phone, I had no way to escape and I was so scared. I didn't know what he was going to do. Luckily, when he came back I managed to knock him out."

"How?" Greg asked. I jumped in my seat—I hadn't been expecting him to speak.

"When he tried to, well, shall we say force his advances on me, I kneed him in the balls and knocked his head against the wall. I grabbed his keys and ran for it."

"Damn it, Kerry, don't tell such ridiculous lies to me," he snapped. "At least honor me with the truth."

"This *is* the truth." I leaned against the desk and looked him in the eye. "I promise you it is. Would I make this up? If I was going to make up a convincing lie, Greg, this wouldn't be it. It sounds ridiculous even to me and I lived it."

He shook his head. "Right, fine, carry on with your story." I could tell from the way he spoke that he still didn't believe me but I carried on.

"I ran away and with the help of a kind old gentleman I got back to the hotel. When I got there I got your message and my luggage and made my way home. You know I tried to contact you then, but you didn't respond. I didn't know what to do so I just got stuck in at work. I didn't have any way to contact you and you were making it clear you didn't want to see me. I wouldn't be here now if I didn't need you. I've been pushed to desperation. Darren rang me just when I got back to the UK and threatened me, not just me, but my business. Since then everything has gone wrong—bad reviews, suppliers pulling out of contracts, visits from the council and Environmental Health, staff leaving. You name it, I've put up with it, but this morning when I reached work it was on fire. The bastard has burnt down Diamonds."

"I'm sorry," he said. "I know how much the club means to you."

I nodded. Tears flooded down my cheeks. I had nothing left, my business was in ruins, my private life was a mess and I couldn't deny it anymore, I couldn't hold it together for even a moment longer. It just flowed out of me in an unstoppable flood of tears and sobs.

"Kerry, oh, Kerry." He sighed and fidgeted in his seat. "I wish I could believe you but it all sounds so far-fetched."

I nodded, gasped in a lungful of air and wiped at my tear-stained cheeks. I wasn't going to make a fool of myself in front of him.

"I'm sorry," I gulped. "I wish I had some proof too, oh, do I. Darren is making my life a misery, Greg, but it's nothing compared to the heartache of losing you."

And so the tears rocked me again. I really wanted to hold it together but I was broken, completely and utterly at the end of my tether. I couldn't stop crying no matter how much I tried.

Greg sat opposite me and said nothing. His jaw was no longer set and his eyes showed concern in their dark depths. He was leaning toward me from his side of the desk but he kept his hands clasped together, almost as if he was holding himself back.

"Okay," he finally spoke. "Okay, I'm going to ask you what may seem to be a weird question right now. Just go with it."

I nodded.

"Which mobile network do you use?"

I'm sobbing my heart out and he wants to sell me a phone package? I shook my head, I couldn't believe that was the motivation to the question really, but it was what jumped to mind first.

"Stamford's," I replied. "I'm already on your network."

"Okay, good. Now, another question. Did Darren ring you on your mobile phone?"

"Yes, he did." I looked up, wiped my cheek with the back of my hand. I was starting to understand what the questions were leading to.

"Okay, okay. I've just got to ring someone and we won't get an immediate answer, but we could, maybe, possibly, be able to prove at least part of your story."

Greg picked up his phone and looked at a piece of paper on his desk. He carefully dialed a number, then opened his desk drawer. He pulled out a box of tissues and pushed them across the wood to me. His first act of kindness since I had walked into his office. I crumpled into tears again.

I didn't usually respond so hysterically to things. I wasn't much of a crier really, but in that office I felt like I cried enough tears to last a lifetime. I tried to get a grip on myself while Greg spoke on the phone.

"Hiya, Trent, I need you to look up something for me. I need you to check the phone records for the account registered to Kerry Matthews. I have the number here." He read out my number from the display on his phone. I felt a weird warmness inside when I realized he'd not deleted me as a contact.

"When did he ring you?" Greg asked. I got out my phone and checked the call logs.

"The twentieth of February at three twenty-eight p.m."

"Did you hear that, Trent? Yeah, three twenty-eight p.m. We need to know who rang and if we can get the call data. I need to hear the content of that call too." He paused, looked up at me and smiled. It was only a brief lifting of his lips but it was a smile all the same.

"Brilliant, thanks, Trent. Treat this as priority, it could be a case for criminal prosecution. Yep, okay, tell me the moment you get it."

Greg put down the phone and looked at me.

"Right, well, you know what I've done. I'm going to try to listen to that call Darren made to you. If it is, as you claim, filled with threats, I will know you're telling the truth, at least partly."

I scanned my memory quickly. That phone call was etched chillingly clearly there. "I think it could prove my whole story, we talked about Venice before he threatened the business."

"It's a slim chance, Kerry, I have to warn you of that. It's not as simple as it sounds to find the info."

"No, I appreciate that, Greg. I just hope it comes through for me."

"I wish I didn't need proof," Greg sighed, "but where he's involved…"

"I know." I nodded, scrunching tissues in my hands. "I really do. I understand but I can't deny it hurts me that you won't take my word for it."

"It hurts me too." He pushed his chair back from the desk. "But I'm a jaded man, Kerry, and although I long to be able to simply trust you, I find that experience has taught me I can't."

"I've never done anything to purposefully hurt you, you know." I got up and followed Greg over to the window that was directly behind his desk. The view over the city was breath-taking. I stood next to him, a few inches between our bodies, and looked out over the metropolis, astounded by its vastness.

"I was scared to death when I went back to the balcony that night and you weren't there. I searched high and low and it was only when I asked the footmen who were on duty by the canal exit that I found out you were okay and that you'd left with Darren. I was relieved and appalled all at once."

I reached out my hand. My knuckles almost brushed his when I decided that touching him might not be my best move.

"I couldn't believe it, but then I saw the CCTV footage and I had to believe what I saw."

"I wasn't happy, Greg, surely you saw that? I wasn't smiling." I wanted to defend myself, which was ridiculous really — I was the victim, after all.

"I didn't see anything past you and him together," Greg replied. "It's all I've been able to see whenever I close my eyes."

He looked toward me. His eyes were lined with gray shadows, his face etched with pain and disappointment.

"I was petrified, Greg. I was being kidnapped." I might have felt a little sympathy for him but I was still angry at him too. He hadn't come to rescue me, no, he hadn't even waited for me. He'd left me stranded in a foreign country and he'd promised never to leave me.

He shrugged.

"I didn't know that. Darren is a bastard, but I didn't think he was capable of that."

"Look." I grabbed Greg's hand. His first reaction was to shake me free but then he held still. I gulped, my senses racked by touching him. "What I need to know right now is can we ever get back together? Even if it's proved that all I've told you is the truth, will you be able to trust me?"

I kept my hand on his, unwilling to pull it back, to lose its warmth, its comfort.

He let out a deep shuddering breath and turned to face me. He caught my other hand in his, held both of them down at my sides and looked deep into my eyes.

"I never wanted to not trust you," he whispered. "I didn't want to believe what I saw, I didn't want to think you were capable of crushing me like that."

I shook my head gently, insistently, tears pooling once more, threatening to fall.

"And now, now I'm faced with the possibility I was wrong. All the pain I've been through, all the sleepless nights, completely self-inflicted. I'm wondering if I've missed something, if I should have examined the footage harder, longer. If I've –" His voice ceased and I stepped forward, wanting to comfort him. "If I've ruined our relationship just because of my own hang-ups, I don't think I'll ever forgive myself. I said I'd never leave you and if you didn't go of your own accord, I did. I broke my promise."

I slipped my hands out of his and stepped forward. I wrapped myself around him and buried my face in his chest. Greg stood poker still as I sobbed against his bright red tie then he encompassed me in his embrace. He stroked my back and rested his chin on the top of my head.

I didn't want to think, I didn't want to remember anything, I didn't want the moment to stop. I was in his arms, I was held in the arms of the man I loved and for the first time in weeks I felt safe.

"I can't do this," he said and pulled back. "I want to, but I can't, I really can't."

I pulled back too. "I know, but I needed that. It's all I've wanted for weeks, I've just felt so alone." Once again, despite my determination not to, I burst into tears.

"Oh, jeez, Kerry, I'm so sorry." He reached out again and pulled me to his chest. I sobbed uncontrollably and he just held me. I was warm, comfortable and content while I was in his arms. Nothing had really changed—when he let me go I'd still be clubless, manless and broken-hearted—but in the safety of his embrace none of that mattered.

"Better?" he asked when the sobbing had subsided.

"Yes," I replied, "though I don't think your shirt will ever be the same again."

He laughed. "Oh good, your sense of humor is still intact. Look, I'm going to call Chester to get home. Do you want a lift?"

"No, it's okay. I'll get the Tube."

"Are you sure?"

I nodded. "Yeah. If I hang around much longer I'm going to try to kiss you and if you resist it'll make me cry again and I swear I haven't got any tears left."

"I won't resist," Greg replied. "I can't resist you."

I didn't wait to think. I pushed myself against him, tipped my head back and kissed him. He did resist for a little while, probably a split second, but from my prone position it felt like forever before his lips moved in sync against mine. I forgot all the heartache, all the loneliness in that kiss. As our lips danced it was like we'd never been parted. He ran his hands down my shoulders and I gripped his hips, holding on for dear life while arousal and desire flooded me.

I wanted him to take me there, up against the window, I wanted to feel his naked flesh against mine but just as I contemplated running my hand inside his shirt my conscience kicked in.

"I'd love to keep going," I panted and licked my lips, "but it's not fair, is it? I'd be using my feminine wiles on you and you're not sure you trust me. I don't want to make it harder for you. I don't want to persuade you with sex."

He nodded, squeezed the tops of my arms and dipped his head to kiss me again. I was taken by surprise and staggered back.

"I trust you, Kerry," he breathed. "I do. I just let my stupid insecurities get in the way. Let me ring Chester. We'll go back to my place, I'll cook us something tasty, we'll drink something fruity and decadent and just catch up. What do you say to that?"

"It sounds really good, Greg, but what happens if – "

"It won't. I'll either get to hear that call or I won't. I don't care now – unless you're confessing undying love to the Scouse gingernut in it there's nothing I could hear to change my mind. I promise. I was stupid, I jumped to conclusions. I don't want to waste any more time thinking about that."

"If I say all right and I come with you, I'm trusting you, really trusting you, because I'm so fragile right now I'm not sure I could take more bad news, honestly, Greg. You broke a promise to me once before. I couldn't take any more."

"There is minimal risk that you've been lying to me all along and I'll discover that and so, we'll be back to square one. It's minimal. If you're telling me the truth, I want you back in my life. I've been miserable without you. I promise to you that I love you and I will try never, ever to be so wilfully stupid in future."

I read the sincerity in his eyes, in the tone of his voice, and I wanted to believe him.

"Okay," I relented. "Let's do it."

Greg rang Chester and I waited by the window. I enjoyed the view. I weighed up what I'd done. I still didn't think that sneaking into Greg's place of work had been my best plan ever, but it had worked, or so it seemed. I knew I should have been unforgiving really.

He had believed the worst of me. He'd distrusted me and left me behind.

I found it hard to judge him for that, though. He'd taken the evidence he had and he'd just jumped to the wrong conclusion. Did it really say much about his relationship with me or was it more about his history with Darren? After all, I had played them off against each other when we first met, so it didn't take a huge leap to get to the conclusion he'd made. I couldn't hate him for that.

"Chester will be here in half an hour. I just need to do a little work before we leave, to set up for tomorrow."

"Okay, no problem." I smiled.

"Do you want a drink or a snack? There's everything you could ever want over there in the corner."

"I'll get myself a drink, thanks."

He wasn't exaggerating. In the corner near the door where I came in was a fridge and it was filled to overflowing with all kinds of things. I pulled out a bottle of water and wandered back over to his desk while I waited.

I changed my mind a little about having a desk job when I looked around Greg's huge office. It was filled with comforts, good views and he clearly had all the communication he wanted at the end of the phone or with the hundreds of other people working in the office block with him.

"Hello, miss." Chester greeted me when we went down to meet him. "Very good to see you again."

"And you, Chester." I smiled when he opened the limo door for me. "Thank you." I slipped in and Greg followed, sitting close next to me and slipping his arm around my shoulders.

"It's good to have you close again," he whispered in my ear. "Have I told you I missed you?"

"I don't remember," I replied with a coy smile. "Say it again."

"I missed you," he repeated and kissed me.

"I missed you too," I replied as I breathed out his soft kiss.

We snuggled in silence for the rest of the journey. I even fell asleep crooked in his arm, held tight to his chest for a while.

"Come on, sleepy head." Greg woke me with a gentle shake. "We've reached home."

I wasn't exactly sure where we were. The house was surrounded by bushes and trees and seemed as far away from central London as it was possible to get. The front door was shiny black and we stepped up half a dozen stone stairs to get to it. The building was square and gray and definitely old. I was quite taken by its grandeur. Inside the décor was matched with its exterior, minimalistic — hardwood floors and light-colored walls with very little extravagant decoration.

I followed Greg through to his kitchen, which was bigger than my whole flat put together, with what seemed like acres of black marble tops and dozens of cupboards and a cooker that looked like it meant business. "Blimey," I exclaimed, "you could cook for an army in here."

"Yeah" — he nodded, then walked over to the fridge — "it does seem a little excessive considering I mostly cook for myself, but I do like the space and I get a cleaner in to tidy up after me, which is even better."

"I don't blame you," I replied.

"So, I've got this salmon in. I was thinking it'd be nice with some Asian-style noodles and veggies, what do you think?"

My stomach grumbled. "That sounds delicious, I don't think I've eaten yet today."

Greg shook his head and tutted. "You really need someone to look after you, don't you?"

I bristled for a moment, my usual fight mode kicking in, then I laughed. "I do, I really do. I'm crap at all the day-to-day domestic stuff."

He laughed and nodded.

It was fun watching Greg cook. It was all so effortless and the things he threw in the wok seemed transformed. A little dash of this, a few pieces of that, some chopped-up veg and boom, there was a hearty, one-pot meal that had me salivating.

"We'll eat in the living room, I'm too tired for formality."

He gave me the bowls and forks and pointed me toward the living room. He followed me with a bottle of white wine and two glasses.

"I know it's the middle of the week but I reckon we both deserve a drop of something mellow, what do you think?"

"I agree wholeheartedly. Make mine a big 'un, I won't be in work tomorrow."

"So, what are you going to do about the club?" he asked.

I settled the bowls on the large glass table and sat on the impressive black leather sofa, which was as comfortable as it was masculine and intimidating. "Oh, I don't know," I sighed. "I'll have to put the insurance claim in as soon as possible, I suppose, but I don't know when I'll hear the verdict on how it was started. If they find it's arson, well, fuck knows when I'll get a payout."

"Can you afford to rebuild without the insurance?" Greg popped the cork out of the bottle and poured two generous measures.

"I suppose it depends on the extent of the damage. I've got some funds. I think I'd need to try and get a loan somehow, but I'll sure as hell scrape together the money if it kills me."

"That's the spirit." He passed me a glass and held his out for a toast. "I won't offend you by offering the money outright, but if you need a loan, come to me, we'll sort out some kind of good deal. I'll get my legal team on it."

"Thank you." I smiled. "I appreciate that. If I need it, I'll let you know. I have to say, the idea of canvassing banks for loans had filled me with dread." We clinked our glasses together and I drank. "Ooh, this is smooth." I moaned.

"It's a favorite of mine," he replied. "I knew you'd like it."

"So, thanks for the offer of help."

"No problem. It's a no-brainer. I know I'll get my investment back, you're so driven."

I nodded. "I've doubted it a time or two recently — it's been one problem after another at work and I've wished I was capable of giving up a time or two."

"You're not going to, though, right?"

"No way." I leaned forward, put down my glass and picked up my bowl of noodle goodness. "I'm not going to let Darren get his way."

The conversation dried up then and as much as I enjoyed the noodles I couldn't take the tension. "Sorry, we should ban his name from conversation."

"No, no, it's okay." Greg shook his head. "Can't let the bastard get us down."

I nodded. "He said you were the bastard, that you nicked his girlfriend or something? He ranted on for ages about it."

"Oh, that old chestnut." Greg dipped his fork into his bowl, twirled up some noodles and ate them before continuing. "I did no such thing. His girl, who he thought was an angel, had neglected to tell me she was seeing my best mate. It was as much a shock to me as it was to him. I was really forgiving back then, so when she said she really loved me, I believed her until I found her in bed with some random exchange student."

"Oh, jeez. You must have thought history was repeating itself."

"A bit" — he nodded — "at first anyway."

"I'm really sorry about that, I shouldn't have led you both on."

"No, no, not your fault. You were honest with us both all along. Either of us could have backed out at any time. The problem's firmly with two pig-headed blokes with more money than sense, not you."

"Well, I'm not sure anyone has a billion pounds' worth of sense." I laughed.

"I certainly don't," he chuckled. We continued eating and drinking, relaxing into each other's company.

"That was good." I patted my stomach, sat back and eased into the comfort of the chair.

"Not bad, even if I do say so myself," he agreed and set his bowl beside mine on the table. He moved back into the sofa. His hand brushed against mine. I extended my fingers and he entwined his between them.

"Mind if I flick on the TV?" he asked.

"No, go ahead." I was full, a little sleepy after the wine and very content just to snuggle where we were for a while.

"The building has been reduced to rubble. The well-known and well-loved bar and restaurant was reported ablaze in the early hours of the morning. Firefighters have only recently put the blaze out. Foul play has not been ruled out and there is a possibility this was a case of arson. Miss Matthews has struggled over recent times with bad reviews and other problems. Some think she may have set light to Diamonds herself to gain the insurance payout."

"Oh, good to see the rumors are already flying." I sighed.

Greg shrugged. "I wouldn't let it get to you, there's always rumors."

"It isn't what they're saying that's upsetting," I said. "It's the pictures. Look at it, Greg, it's in ruins."

He squeezed my hand comfortingly. "I know, but you'll build it back up again. See it as an opportunity. Surely there's something you've always wanted to change? Well, now you can put it into the new plan."

"Wow, that's major-league optimism. I wish I could see past the destruction."

"It's still raw," Greg replied. "You're still grieving and so you're allowed to be irrational. The optimism will replace that eventually."

"I suppose." I sighed again. The news had moved on to something else but I could still see the ruined, smoke-blackened bricks and the fresh air where windows and walls and the doors should have been.

"You've really been through it, haven't you, sweetheart?" He turned to me and pulled me into an embrace. "I'm sorry I've not been around for you because of my stupid selfishness. I'm sorry I've hurt you."

"Don't worry." I held him tight. "We've sorted it out now and we can't change the past, can we? But we can influence the future."

"True." He kissed my neck gently. "That's very true. I'm going to do all I can to make the future better."

"You're going to buy me a lifetime's worth of chocolate?" I pressed my hands to his cheeks and pulled him up to kiss his lips.

"If that's what you want." He smiled.

"Oh, you're going to give me what I want?" I questioned, still holding his face in my hands.

"Definitely," he whispered, his voice raspy. The tone vibrated deep in my stomach, making it flip.

"That's what I like to hear."

"So, what do you want?" he asked.

"You," I whispered, the word catching in my throat, not because I didn't want to utter it but because I wanted it so very much.

"You've got me," he replied, his smile gentle and heart-warming and even more warming when he pressed it to my lips.

I melted into him, rolled my touch down to his shoulders and his chest. He grasped my shoulders, then his strong grip lessened and he moved his touch down into the center of my body, cupping my breasts, eliciting a gasp from me as he shifted his hands down to my hips. I felt lightheaded and it wasn't from the wine. His touch intoxicated me. After being so miserable for so long I couldn't believe he was with me again, making me feel so good.

As Greg removed my top, his hands slipping under the material and hefting it up, I moved my arms to accommodate him. When my hands were freed I dropped them to his chest and fiddled nervously with the buttons there as he captured my mouth once more with his. The gentle scrape of end-of-the-day stubble on my cheek added to the arousal.

It took a few moments to release the buttons, and I left the shirt hanging on his shoulders and enjoyed the feel of his hard lines beneath my fingers. I reveled in his heat beneath my fingertips, teased his nipples, enjoyed the crinkle of response and ruffled the dark hairs across his abs. I followed them down over his stomach to reach the fastening of his trousers.

He was equally busy undoing my bra strap. His big hands on my back warmed my blood as he guided the material off my shoulders—leading me to stop my ministrations for a moment—then grabbed at my revealed breasts and kneaded them enthusiastically. The roaring rumbling he made in the back of his throat rolled through me, urging me on to release him from the bottom half of his smart suit.

I pushed forward and he collapsed back along the length of the sofa. I leaned over him and trailed kisses down from his upturned lips, caught in a surprised smile, and onto his neck then lower across his chest. I took in details of his contours and lavished love on him. I noted a mole just above his left nipple, and the flush that bloomed across his chest in his arousal. I could feel the very thick, very obvious evidence that he was turned on as my pelvis pressed down on his crotch. I was eager to feel more of him, I wanted the joy of his erection inside me, but I didn't rush. I wanted to take my time. I wanted to remember everything in detail.

He impatiently bumped his hips as I meandered down over his body but this time I was in control and I wasn't going to give in. I finally reached the band

and belt at the top of his trousers. I balanced myself on my elbows and worked frantically to release his belt and zip. My heart thudded rhythmically and I fizzed with stored energy. I was aware of every little thing. The cool air above me, his hot body below. The clink of his belt as it fell loosely to his side, the just perceptible whoosh of the material slipping down his legs and the creak of the expensive leather as our bodies shifted.

I could hear his breathing under mine, and the TV babbling in the background. I wasn't paying attention to what was said, though, I was concentrating on revealing his cock. It sprang eagerly into sight when I eased his trousers and boxers down his thighs. I drank in the visual first, reacquainting myself with his length, the unique crick that I then teased my fingers down, reacquainting myself with its shape and heft.

I drank in his scent, masculine and musky and somehow amplified by the richness of the leather beneath us. My mouth watered and I licked my lips. Greg reached out and desperately grabbed at my shoulders, trying to hurry me along. I resisted, enjoying teasing him, not wanting to rush a single moment.

I dipped my lips to his balls, which wrinkled pleasantly under my kiss, then I continued on to the tautness of his erection. I kissed lightly then nibbled the straining flesh, running up higher with my kisses and licks, he moaned continually until I reached his tip and sank my lips around him.

"Oh, yeah," he gasped as I sank my mouth lower, then retracted it. Tasting and enjoying the stretch of his dick, the rigidity of it against my tongue. I lovingly licked and sucked, concentrating fully on giving him pleasure. He gripped my ponytail, wrapping the loose curls tight around his fist to control the rise and fall of my ministration. I surrendered to it, eager to please him, then unexpectedly he pulled me off him. My lips popped and I groaned my frustration.

"I have to fuck you," he growled. "I need to—your mouth—oh, it was amazing but I don't want to come like that, not right now. I need to be inside you."

I didn't argue. I moved back into a seated position and he pushed himself up. Greg lunged forward and pushed me back with his hands and his ferocious kisses. I undid my jeans and pushed them down my legs with my knickers and kicked them off as they pooled at my ankles.

"You're so beautiful," he crooned between harsh kisses, "so gorgeous, so amazing." We scrambled together. I twisted my body round and insinuated myself so that my thighs were split around him. He moved back, pulled his knees up beneath him and waited, poised to plunge into me.

I lay panting, thighs splayed, breasts bouncing in time to my breathing. He watched me. It was his turn to tease. I wanted him to touch me, to fuck me savagely but he just sat and watched me. His gaze traveled down from my face, to my heaving chest, down over my soft stomach and to my crotch. I'd drunk in his details and he was doing the same. I wondered what he was taking note of—the color of my aroused nipples, the curl of my pubic hair, the way one of my intimate lips protrudes farther than the other or the way they plump with blood when I'm turned on.

Greg finally reached out and touched me just at the top of my thigh. I watched intently as he trailed his fingers into the damp folds of my pussy. He stroked and pushed until his fingertip entered me, leaving it there as I desperately clutched with my muscles to pull him deeper.

He withdrew that finger, his pointer, then lifted it to his mouth and sucked it in. I felt sparks of pleasure in my pussy when I imagined him licking my juice from the source. I shivered with desire, my skin prickling with anticipation. Ever so slowly he withdrew it, licked his lips and lifted up from resting back on his heels. He scooched forward until his cock was brushing against my lips.

Greg curved his lithe body over me, his hands resting on the arm of the sofa just above my head, and he pushed forward. He pressed just below my entrance then swept up and his tip slipped in, just. He held there, looking down and deep into my eyes. I felt like I was falling into his gaze, like I was becoming part of him.

I didn't know what he saw in me. I hoped it was all the love inside me, not just the raw lust, because he pressed forward and I opened for him, pulled him tight into my intimate embrace. As his cock was fully sheathed within me I grabbed at his sides, holding him, reassuring myself it was real.

He moved in and out slowly, rhythmically with great control. I closed my eyes and absorbed every throb, every slip and slide of our entwining. It was more than sex, it was deeper and more sensual. I felt myself healing as we moved in time together. All that had been out of balance, all that hadn't been right in the past weeks clicked into place. I was whole again.

I fluttered my eyes open and Greg was still staring down at me. "I love you." I had to say the words, they were pent up inside and had to be released.

"I love you too," he responded and bent his arms so he could reach down and kiss me. His cock stilled inside me and I didn't want the moment to end.

"Touch yourself," he demanded when he pulled back. "I want to feel you come around me, I want to feel you squeezing me as you explode."

I moved my hand from where I gripped his side and slid it between our bodies. He lifted slightly so I could extend my finger between my lips and to rest on my plump clit. I slipped it lower and gathered up some of the silken liquid that flowed from our joining and lifted it to coat my nub.

I rubbed up and down, and he thrust in time. I was taken with the rhythm, absorbed by the synchronicity of our joining. We worked perfectly together and as the pressure built inside me, the intensity of his thrusts heightened. As I brought myself to the brink of orgasm he copied me.

The first spark bathed my clit in pleasure and my body reacted by pulling Greg deeper inside. I moaned, my chest vibrated, my skin tightened and the force of a love-fueled orgasm racked my being. He came then, almost at exactly the same moment, maybe a split second later when I throbbed around him. He seemed to expand and retract to the same rhythm.

I rode the feeling, gasped and panted as the explosion stilled and I came to a standstill beneath him. He slipped down, his cock leaving me, his head rolling into the crook of my shoulder. We snuggled together then, needing the comfort of each other's embrace. We were raw and the contentment of the sexual joining was only the start of mending our relationship.

"Stay with me," he whispered after the silence between us had become too much.

"Okay," I replied eagerly.
"I need you."
"I need you too."

Chapter Twelve

The next day I woke in Greg's bed. He wasn't there but he'd left a note on his pillow.

I've gone to work. Chester knows you're still here. Feel free to stay, make yourself at home, I'll ring you later. Love you, Greg.
P.S. you snore so prettily when you sleep.

I shrieked with rage then laughed. I was fairly certain I didn't snore and I was also pretty certain he was trying to wind me up. I pushed myself out from beneath the feather-light duvet and stretched out the cricks of a night's sleep.

I slipped my feet into the deep pile of the scarlet carpet and levered myself from the curved, dark wood bed. I walked toward the door on the opposite side of the room from where I had entered and sure enough it was a bathroom. It was magnificently clean—the marbled tiles and the bright white tops all sparkled. I leaped into the shower and spent some time working out how to use it. There were several jets and I loved feeling the water hitting me from all different angles. I wasted a good long time in there before wrapping myself in a huge, fluffy white towel and heading back to the bedroom.

It was a very masculine room, basic but clearly expensive. There were practical pieces of furniture, beautiful in their simplicity, and plain white paint on the walls.

I slipped my bra and knickers on, then my jeans and top. They'd been left on the ottoman at the end of the bed. I hoped Greg had collected them for me, I wasn't sure I wanted Chester or another member of staff to be so intimately acquainted with my underwear.

I opened the curtains and looked over the tops of the trees into the general busy jumble of houses and offices of a London skyline. I admired the unique beauty of my city and was pulled from it when my mobile phone vibrated in my pocket. I took it out and after checking the caller pressed a button and lifted it to my ear.

"Hello."

"Hey, Kerry, sleep well?"

"Yes, thanks, and I don't snore." I giggled.

"Hmm, well, if you say so." He laughed.

"I do," I retorted.

"Fair enough. I was just ringing to see if you were up, I've got something here you might want to see. You up to coming to my place of work again?"

"Yeah, sure, erm, where's the nearest Tube station to your house? I don't have a clue where I am, you know."

Greg chortled heartily. "Chester's there, he'll give you a lift."

"Oh, right."

"I'll ring him and let him know you'll be waiting in the hall in five minutes, all right?"

"Yeah, sure."

"Good, see you soon."

I shook my head as I put the phone back in my pocket. I still had a lot to get used to—Greg's billionaire lifestyle was still quite foreign to me.

Chester was waiting in the hall when I found my way downstairs. He smiled broadly and escorted me into the limo then on to Greg's work. This time the receptionist led me straight to the main lift when I told her my name.

"I'm sorry about yesterday," I apologized as we waited. "You were so nice to me and I took advantage of that."

"Oh, don't worry." She smiled. "I was hoping you'd notice the opportunity. Mr Stamford has been miserable without you."

We went straight into Greg's office and this time he beamed widely.

"Ah, Kerry, I'm glad you're here. I recorded the news, I thought you'd be interested in it."

Greg beckoned me over to where he sat and slapped his lap. I took a seat with him on his side of the desk and looked over to the wall opposite. Greg pointed a remote and the white wall sprang into life as a TV screen.

"Darren Bennett has been helping the police with their enquiries this morning in regards to charges of kidnap and arson, amongst other more minor charges of fraud and bribery."

I looked at Greg and his gaze was fixed on the screen. He was smiling broadly. I glanced back and paid attention once more to the report.

"Mr Bennett was caught out when a phone call he made to Diamonds bar owner Kerry Matthews was intercepted and reported to the police. They are continuing to investigate the allegations, believing that the alleged threatening phone call connected him to several counts of fraud as well as arson and kidnap."

I watched lights flashing and Darren stepped out of an office, flanked either side by police officers. He was pressed into the back of a police car and the footage then flicked to the burnt-out shell of Diamonds.

Greg stopped the footage with another click.

"So, you found the call then?"

"Oh, yeah." He nodded. "I got a call from Trey at seven this morning about it. So we got straight down to business, reported it to the police. That's okay by you, right?"

I nodded emphatically.

"And the police did the rest. They're going to question the staff at Michael's in Venice and check the other calls Darren's made. He's not going to get away with what he did to you, Kerry."

"Good." I sighed. I could feel tears bubbling up inside. I wanted to cry with the relief.

"It'll be all right now." He cuddled me tightly against him. "I want to apologize again for not believing you—"

"Don't," I interrupted. "It's in the past. Let's not dwell on it. We're together now and that idiot is going to end up behind bars. You caught the bad guy and got the girl in the end, it's the perfect fairy tale. I think that makes you my prince."

"And you're my princess, Kerry. I'm so lucky to have you. I love you so much."

"I love you too, Greg." I squeezed him tightly as I flicked my eyelashes to prevent myself from crying. It was all happening so quickly. I had Greg back and it felt so good and now the black cloud that hung over me was banished too. Darren was going to pay for what he had done and, almost more importantly, Greg knew the truth. All the residual worry that I had held on to dissipated. I could have danced with joy I was so happy.

Greg coughed and wriggled in the seat beneath me. I shook myself from my thoughts and looked at him.

"I was going to do something that night on the balcony and I really want to do it now instead," he stated, his voice far more confident than the look on his face. He seemed nervous and I wondered what he *was* going to do.

He leaned forward and opened a drawer in his big desk. He pulled out a little black velvet box.

"I know this is probably not the most romantic setting, but I need to ask you this question now because, Kerry, you complete me and I don't want to lose you ever again."

He clicked open the box and inside there was a ring, sparkling with diamonds. I gasped and threw my hand over my mouth as tears dripped down my cheeks.

"Kerry, will you marry me?"

I was completely overwhelmed but I managed to nod and he bent his head to kiss me. I was completely enveloped in his embrace and I didn't want to be anywhere else.

"Yes," I gasped out as we parted. "Yes, I'll marry you."

He slipped the ring from the box and onto my finger. He held my hand flat in his and we admired the shiny ring together.

"Yours forever," I sighed. "I don't think I've ever been happier in my life."

Greg squeezed me tightly to him.

"I know I haven't, Kerry, you *are* my life."

I knew then that Greg was the only man I'd ever want and I'm sorry, ladies, but I'm never going to share him nicely. He's all mine.

About the Author

Victoria Blisse is a mother, wife, Christian, Manchester United fan and award winning erotica author. She is also the editor of several Bigger Briefs collections, and the co-editor of the fabulous Smut Alfresco and Smut in the City and Smut by the Sea Anthologies.

She is equally at home behind a laptop or a cooker and she loves to create stories, poems, cakes and biscuits that make people happy. She was born near Manchester, England and her northern English quirkiness shows through in all of her stories.

Passion, love and laughter fill her works, just as they fill her busy life.

Victoria Blisse loves to hear from readers. You can find her contact information, website details and author profile page at http://www.totallybound.com.

Totally Bound Publishing

Home of Erotic Romance